SHERLOCK HOLMES AND THE RULE OF NINE

Recent Titles by Barrie Roberts

SHERLOCK HOLMES AND THE RULE OF NINE

Edited & Annotated by Barrie Roberts
from a manuscript believed to be the
work of
John H. Watson, MD

This first world edition published in Great Britain 2003 by
SEVERN HOUSE PUBLISHERS LTD of
9–15 High Street, Sutton, Surrey SM1 1DF.
This first world edition published in the USA 2004 by
SEVERN HOUSE PUBLISHERS INC of
595 Madison Avenue, New York, N.Y. 10022.

British Library Cataloguing in Publication Data

Roberts, Barrie, 1939-
   Sherlock Holmes and the rule of nine
  1.   Holmes, Sherlock (Fictitious character) - Fiction
  2.   Watson, John H. (Fictitious character) - Fiction
  3.   Racketeering - England - London - Fiction
  4.   Detective and mystery stories
  I.   Title
  823.9'14 [F]

ISBN 0-7278-6004-6

Typeset by Palimpsest Book Production Ltd.,
Polmont, Stirlingshire, Scotland.
Printed and bound in Great Britain by
MPG Books Ltd., Bodmin, Cornwall.

Editor's Introduction

I have explained elsewhere how I inherited a quantity of manuscripts which appear to be the work of John H. Watson, MD, chronicler of the cases of Sherlock Holmes. They may have belonged to my maternal grandfather, who was both a medical man and a colleague of Watson's in the Medical Corps during the Great War.

I have edited a number of these for publication, including *Sherlock Holmes and the Railway Maniac* (Constable, 1994; A & B Books, 2001), *Sherlock Holmes and the Devil's Grail* (Constable, 1995; A & B Books, 2000), *Sherlock Holmes and the Man from Hell* (Constable, 1997; Linford Mystery Library, 2000), *Sherlock Holmes and the Royal Flush* (Constable, 1998), *Sherlock Holmes and the Harvest of Death* (Constable, 1999), *Sherlock Holmes and the Crosby Murder* (Constable & Robinson, 2002, Carroll & Graff, 2002), 'The Mystery of the Addleton Curse' (in the *Mammoth Book of New Sherlock Holmes Adventures*, Robinson Books, 1998), 'The Disappearance of Daniel Question', 'The Abbas Parva Tragedy', 'The Affair of the Christmas Jewel' (*Strand Magazine*, USA, April & December 2001, December 2002) and the present text.

No undisputed specimen of John Watson's handwriting survives, which makes authentication of the manuscripts difficult. Internal evidence is confused by Watson's habit of substituting names, places and sometimes dates, but in my notes at the end of the manuscript I record some of my attempts to check out aspects of the narrative.

One

The Game May Be Afoot

I would not have my readers believe that the career of my friend Mr Sherlock Holmes was one of unalloyed success, nor, to be fair, would he. In his striving to refine further the ratiocinative processes which he applied in his enquiries he was his own sternest critic, and there were certain cases which he never mentioned without adding that he had failed in them, or had made certain errors. Often he was referring to matters where his client had been well content, but Holmes was not, himself, satisfied with his handling of the problem.

One case which I knew irked him was the affair of the Vatican Cameos, a matter of which I had little recollection for I was otherwise engaged at the time of my friend's involvement in the case. Holmes never mentioned the matter without remarking that his enquiry had been frustrated and that it should have been possible to obtain a conviction.

1895 was a busy year for Holmes, as I have already recorded. It was also a year of unremitting cold in the early months, so much so that a blue moon was seen over London and skaters on the frozen Thames witnessed a rare appearance of the Northern Lights over the capital in February. These events were considered to be omens and there was much speculation as to their possible meaning. No clearly identifiable event could be associated with the omens and, when the weather warmed, the portents were forgotten. It may be that the warnings were to Sherlock Holmes, that a singularly frustrating case was about to take up his efforts.

*   *   *

1

We sat at breakfast one morning in the summer of '95, Holmes still in one of his gaudier dressing gowns, surrounded by the usual litter which he made of the morning papers.

'Do you recall,' he asked suddenly, 'the Vatican Cameos affair?'

'I have no clear recollection of it,' I admitted.

'No.' He smiled. 'I remember that it occurred some seven years ago, when you were newly wed and I saw little of you.'

I nodded. 'I know that you have always expressed your dissatisfaction at the outcome,' I remarked.

'Dissatisfaction is far too mild a word, Watson. My enquiries led to an inescapable conclusion, yet my views as to the identity of one of the criminals caused a sudden loss of interest in the matter, as a result of which a deep-dyed villain continues to masquerade as a man of principle and piety, an ugly gang of blackmailers, thieves and worse is still at large, and the cameos – which are priceless – are still missing.'

He stood up and went to his pipe rack, selecting a short briar and filling it energetically.

'What was the importance of the cameos?' I asked.

He lit his pipe and puffed at it heartily before falling into an armchair.

'They are not,' he said, 'strictly cameos in the classical sense. It was, I believe, the newspapers who applied that term, but they are, in fact, exquisite miniature portraits painted on ivory. They are unique, and their history is bound up with the history of this country, Watson. They belonged to the Morence family in the West of England. It appears that a member of that family commissioned them from the great miniaturist painter Thomas Wenton at the time of the religious persecutions three hundred years ago.'

'What were the subjects?' I asked.

'The subjects were five of the itinerant priests who travelled the country bringing the sacraments to Catholic families in secret. All five of them were subsequently captured, tortured and executed.'

'It seems unwise of them to have had their portraits painted,' I remarked.

'Quite so,' he agreed, 'but the Morence who commissioned Wenton believed – rightly as events have proved – that the Roman faith would not always be proscribed and that the men who risked their lives to carry the sacraments to his family in that dark time deserved recognition of their courage and devotion. It was with that in mind that he persuaded them to sit for Wenton.'

'He must have kept them very safe,' I observed. 'Surely the government's spies would have been delighted to have good likenesses of five of the men they sought.'

'He kept them so safely that they were thought to have been lost or destroyed until a few years ago. When Morence died, his will provided that his eldest son should take the cameos to Rome, as a gift to the Vatican in honour of the five sitters. Unhappily, his son had predeceased him, and the whereabouts of the cameos was unknown to any other member of the family, so the bequest could not be carried out. Until a few years ago, there were many who believed that Morence had changed his mind and destroyed the paintings, lest they fall into Protestant hands.'

'How did they come to light?' I asked.

Holmes drew on his pipe. 'In 1886 the Morence family fell on hard times and was forced to dispose of a large part of their family estates, most particularly the old family house at Newton Morence. In the course of rebuilding the old house, the new owner's workmen broke into one of those concealed compartments which are a commonplace of Catholic houses of that period.'

'A priest's hole,' I volunteered.

'Precisely, Watson, and one previously unknown to the modern family. It proved to contain some items of religious plate, themselves of no little value, a quantity of priestly garments, and the Vatican Cameos.'

'Extraordinary!' I exclaimed.

Holmes smiled. 'I wonder, Watson, not so much at the

myriad wonderful and significant items that are carried away in the tide of time, but at how many of them are subsequently deposited further along the strand.'

'If the family were reduced to selling their old home, I should have thought that the discovery of the cameos would have put all their financial worries behind them,' I observed.

'They might, indeed,' he agreed, 'but the Morence family had kept to their ancestors' faith and wished to see the bequest honoured, though they saw no reason for not selling the handsome and valuable ritual items which were found with the cameos. They announced that the cameos would go to Rome, as intended, and suitable, if elaborate, arrangements were made.'

'If these cameos were as rare as you suggest, Holmes, it seems to me that very elaborate precautions should have been taken to protect them until they were safe in the Vatican,' I commented.

'Oh, there is no doubt that they are priceless,' said Holmes, 'because of their artistic merit, because of their historic significance and because of their symbolism to the faithful. As it happened, the elaborations were concerned with the ceremony of the handing over, rather than the security of the cameos.'

'How was that?' I asked.

He puffed at his briar. 'Newton Morence having passed out of the hands of the Morence family,' he said, 'Lord Farrismount offered the ancient and ornate chapel at his country seat as a suitable site for the handing over and blessing of the cameos, the Farrismounts being descended from the same Morence who had first commissioned them. The Pope, who had expressed his delight at the discovery of the cameos, appointed Cardinal Tosca – the most senior of his Cardinal Secretaries – as his Special Emissary, who was to come to Britain, take possession of the cameos and return them safely to the Vatican. All this was widely reported in the newspapers, as was the fact that the cameos, by consent of the Pope and the Morence family, would be displayed in the British Museum for four weeks before they left our shores for ever.'

'There was an incident,' I recalled. 'Somebody attempted—'

'Precisely, Watson. A lunatic preacher, called Cravat, was arrested at the Museum after an attempt to daub the cameos with orange paint.'

'Presumably,' I commented, 'as a mark of disapproval from the Orangemen of Ulster?'

'Indeed', he said. 'Fortunately the cameos were not damaged, Cravat was arrested and, after a tediously loud and semi-literate speech to the Justices, was sentenced to three months' imprisonment. He, we can be sure, played no part in what followed.'

He drew on his pipe before continuing. 'Lord Farrismount's estate lies in the West Country and thither, on the eve of the ceremony, went the great and good of the Roman Church. The Cardinal Archbishop of Westminster was there, with his colleagues from Glasgow and Dublin and all of the senior hierarchy of the Church in these islands, as well as many visiting clergy from the Continent. Diehard bigots of Cravat's ilk were loud in their condemnations, seeing the ceremony – rightly – as a triumphal statement by their ancient enemies.'

'All this must have attracted a great deal of publicity. I would have thought it difficult to steal the cameos in such circumstances,' I remarked.

'Indeed,' he said. 'The Reverend Dr Cravat's colleagues encamped about the railway station for days, declaring that they would fight every inch of the way to Lord Farrismount's door to capture the cameos and to prevent what they called "these Papist icons" and "these memorials of traitors" from being made the centrepiece of a "satanic festival". In the circumstances, a heavy police presence was established at the station, the road was cordoned all the way to Farrismount Hall, and officers of the Royal Irish Constabulary were imported to both London and the West Country, so as to identify the more prominent troublemakers among Cravat's supporters.'

'And this was not sufficient?' I said.

He shook his head. 'The British Museum removed the cameos from public exhibition on the afternoon before the ceremony. A party of plain-clothes detectives took them, in a small attaché case, to the home of the Cardinal Archbishop in London, where they reposed in a safe overnight. It was agreed that to accompany them to Farrismount with any large party would merely draw attention, so a single individual was picked, a young priest, who was to travel in lay clothing with the cameos in a commercial traveller's bag early on the following day. On his arrival at the Halt for Farrismount, he was to be met with a strong guard who would convoy him by back roads into the estate.'

'It all sounds sensible,' I remarked.

'Oh, eminently so, Watson. It would have been wiser to post plain-clothes men at each station and halt, so that the courier could give them some sign that he was unmolested, but that was not done and the result was murder and robbery.'

'What actually happened?' I asked.

'When the train reached the halt for Farrismount Hall, the courier failed to appear. A search revealed his dead body in a Third Class compartment. He had been shot twice in the head. Of the Vatican Cameos there was no sign.'

He paused while I absorbed the facts. 'Was it a corridor carriage?' I enquired at last.

He shook his head. 'It was thought safer to use an old-fashioned carriage, so that no one could enter the courier's compartment while the train was in motion.'

'Then how was it done?' I exclaimed.

'With regrettable ease,' said Holmes. 'It was equally easy to reconstruct, with hindsight. Three men, of whom we have only a sketchy description, purchased Third Class tickets at Basingstoke and boarded the same carriage as the courier, taking the compartment next to his. I believe that, at Bennings Halt, one of them left their compartment on the side furthest from the platform. Clinging to the open door and standing on the carriage's footboard, he would see that the courier was seated in the corner seat nearest to him. Before the courier could rise to reach the communication cord, the two shots were fired through the window of the compartment. The rest was simplicity itself.'

'But surely,' I said, 'someone else on the train would have become aware of what was happening!'

'Immediately after Bennings Halt the line bends in a sharp, left-hand curve, through which trains must travel slowly and which makes it nearly impossible to see anything far ahead or behind on the train. The murder was most probably effected there. Once the courier was dead, the killer could enter the compartment, shut the door and search it at will, while his colleagues closed the door of their compartment. In a very short space of time there would have been nothing for any observer, on or off the train, to notice, except perhaps a broken windowpane.'

'And how did the perpetrators escape?' I asked.

'Very simply,' he replied. 'The three tickets taken at Basingstoke were handed in at Salisbury. The three men caught the next up train and were gone, long before any alarm had been spread.'

'But surely – the up train could have been stopped and searched?'

'Oh, it was. Before it reached London, but they had already left it at Basingstoke and from the moment they walked through the ticket gate at Basingstoke they disappeared completely.'

'Outrageous!' I exclaimed. 'An innocent man – a priest – shot dead while carrying out his duty, and a great treasure looted!'

'It is the killing that galls me, Watson. They were three and armed. They might have entered that compartment and threatened the courier into handing over the cameos, but they chose instead to shoot him like a dog. That is why I am determined to locate the cameos and trace the person responsible for their theft.'

'You were unsuccessful at the time,' I said. 'Why was that?'

'I was instructed by Lord Farrismount when the police enquiry had got nowhere. I reached an early conclusion that the criminals knew altogether too much about how the cameos were to be transported. That information, it seems, was most likely to have come from only one person, who had complete control of the arrangements.'

He paused, and the light slowly dawned on me. 'Cardinal Tosca?' I exclaimed incredulously. 'Surely not!'

'Why not?' he demanded. 'No one else could have tipped off the thieves so completely. Tosca made the final arrangements with young Father Grant himself.'

'But why would a man like the Cardinal do such a thing?' I argued.

Holmes drew on his pipe and shook his head slowly. 'Watson, Watson. There is no special class of man that makes a villain. Cardinals and Kings, Popes and Emperors have all, on occasions, shown themselves to be as corrupt, as ruthless, as venal, as cowardly as the meanest denizen of our foulest slum.'

'I suppose you're right,' I agreed reluctantly. 'But he cannot have stolen the cameos himself, can he?'

'Certainly not,' agreed Holmes, 'but he may have been persuaded by some means to collaborate with those who did.'

'What makes you return to the matter now?' I asked.

He smiled, a narrow humourless expression which I had never known to bode his quarry any good. 'This morning's papers reveal that Cardinal Tosca has returned to Britain for what is described as a personal visit. The game may be afoot again, Watson!'

Two

A Matter of Insurance

I knocked my pipe out against the fire grate while I reflected on my friend's narrative.

'I recognize,' I said, 'that you would have difficulty in convicting Tosca without the co-operation of his Church, the more so since he returned to the Vatican, but what of the cameos themselves? Surely, the only reason to steal them would be in order to sell them, and an attempt to put them on the market would become known.'

He shook his head. 'Not so, Watson. It is nearly twenty years since Adam Worth stole the Devonshire portrait, but it has never been offered for sale. Indeed, my private information indicates that Worth either keeps the painting in his personal possession or has it secreted where only he can recover it.'

'Why would he do that?'

'For Worth the game is often its own reward. The mere taking of the painting makes his name a byword. As to why he holds on to it, only he knows the answer. It has been made plain to him that the insurers would be willing to reach an accommodation with him, but he refuses to deal with them.'

'Are they not, by so doing, compounding his felony?' I enquired.

'Oh, indeed,' he agreed, 'but, having paid out an enormous sum in compensation, the painting now belongs to them. One can understand why they would seek to recover it by whatever means. Besides, since the inception of the business, insurers have never concerned themselves much with honesty or the law.'

'Were the Vatican Cameos insured?' I asked.

'Certainly, Watson. As soon as they were discovered, the Morence family had them covered for a very great sum indeed.'

'And have those insurers sought to deal with the thieves?'

'It is rather more delicate when the theft involves murder, but the company's investigators have assured me that they have put the word about that they would deal with anyone not personally involved in the killing of Father Grant. They have had no response and they claim to have no idea as to the whereabouts of the cameos.'

An idea occurred to me. 'What about Worth?' I said. 'This seems to match his behaviour with the Devonshire portrait. Might he not have the Vatican Cameos?'

'Worth?' he exclaimed. 'No, not he. Adam Worth is a criminal genius of the stature of the unlamented Moriarty, but he lacks the late Professor's cold-blooded ruthlessness. Worth eschews violence. He might well have seen the cameos as a worthy target, but there would have been no bloodshed.'

'Bloodshed would not have stopped Moriarty,' I remarked.

'Moriarty,' said my friend, with a stern expression, 'is dead. I saw him die at the Reichenbach.'

'I was merely remarking that, had he survived the Reichenbach Falls, it is the sort of thing that he might have done.'

'A completely fruitless speculation on the possibility of what a dead man might do if he were not dead. I wonder sometimes Watson whence your vein of whimsy and romance springs.'

A knock heralded Mrs Hudson.

'I beg your pardon, Mr Holmes,' she said, 'but one of your lads has just delivered this, saying that it was most urgent.'

She passed Holmes a grubby scrap of paper, which he unfolded and read, dismissing our housekeeper with his thanks.

'It seems,' he told me, 'that another game is afoot. Come, Watson. Let us dress and be about our business.'

*   *   *

I had grown so used to following my friend's lead that it was some half an hour later, as our cab made its way northwards, that it occurred to me to question our errand. Holmes made no reply, simply passing me the paper he had received. The grubby scrap bore a few words in clumsily scrawled indelible pencil:

HE AS GOT BARS UP TODAY. TOMMY

It made no sense to me, and I said so.

'I have been observing,' he explained, 'certain recent patterns in the city.'

'Patterns?' I said. 'Of bars?' I was now even more confused.

'In part, Watson. In part. I have told you before, that any investigation should begin from the examination of patterns. If the official police would pay attention to my methods they might be better able to fulfil their primary function of preventing crime, instead of allowing it to be committed and then trailing along after the perpetrator.'

'But what have bars and patterns to do with crime?'

'I have observed,' he said, 'that there has been, in recent weeks, a steady stream of bizarre incidents reported in the press which share one feature in common – they have all been accidents to the premises or vehicles of small shopkeepers, some of them extremely bizarre.'

'What sort of thing?' I asked.

'Oh, a paper bag of live mice flung into a ladies' hairdressing salon, a pack of stray dogs led to the open door of a butcher's shop by what seems to have been aniseed, that sort of thing. In addition, there have been an inordinate number of burglaries and fires at similar premises and an increase in the number of shops that now protect their premises with iron bars.'

'That seems only sensible to me,' I remarked. 'If burglars or arsonists are at work it seems reasonable to take precautions.'

'Oh, indubitably,' said Holmes, 'but the singular feature of the affair is that those who take precautions are almost invariably the subject of disasters afterwards.'

11

'That merely shows that they were right to be cautious,' I said.

He snorted. 'If butchers and bakers and candlestick makers can foretell the future so accurately, my profession will soon become redundant, as will your own hobby of betting on sporting events!'

'Then what do you think is going on?' I asked.

'It is, I believe, a matter of insurance.'

'Insurance?' I exclaimed. 'You mean these incidents are engineered by the shopkeepers so as to claim against their insurance?'

'No, no,' he said. 'That is a regular and common practice, which the insurance companies usually detect very quickly. It swells whenever there is a slump in trade and dwindles in times of prosperity. No, it is not that. Rather the reverse.'

'You have confused me entirely, Holmes,' I admitted.

'I apologize,' he said. 'Now, you are, as I remarked, a betting man, Watson. When you believe that a specific horse is most likely to win a race, you enter into an agreement with a bookmaker, whereby he will pay you a sum of money if your horse wins, correct?'

I nodded and he went on.

'Insurance operates in exactly the same way. If you believe that your house may be burned down, you enter into an agreement with an insurer, whereby he will pay you a sum of money if your house does burn down. It is, quite simply, another bet, is it not?'

'I can see that,' I said, 'but I don't see how it connects with the situation you described earlier.'

'With your interest in antiquities, Watson, you cannot be unaware of the so-called "fire marks" that still decorate many old buildings.'

'Of course,' I said. 'A leaden plaque with the emblem of an insurance company and often a policy number. They were placed on buildings in the days when insurance companies ran the only fire brigades, before the institution of municipal brigades.'

'And what was their purpose?' Holmes demanded.

'Why, to show an insurance company's fire crew whether a particular building was insured with their company.'

'Precisely,' he agreed. 'So that, if the burning premises were not under their protection, they could save their effort and let them burn. This served as a useful lesson to those who failed to insure their property or adopted the protection of a company without a prompt fire brigade.'

'I understand all that,' I said, 'but I still do not see what you are driving at.'

He smiled. 'Bear with me a little longer, Watson. We regard with distaste the conduct of those commercial brigades in standing aside while life and property were destroyed, but there was a darker aspect to it yet.'

'What was that?' I asked.

'Those same insurance-company marks on houses and shops served as an indicator to the more unscrupulous insurers, identifying premises insured by their competitors which they could set alight with impunity. Thus, the clients of some companies would suffer fires and a popular conception would arise that the best protection from fire was a policy with a particular firm of insurers.'

'That's scandalous!' I exclaimed.

'It is, nevertheless, true, Watson, and something like it is going on in London at present.'

'You mean—?'

'I mean,' he said, 'that small tradesmen are being confronted with a demand to pay for protection of their business. Those who pay are protected. Those who refuse, and increase the security of their premises, are marked as examples and strange disasters occur to them, which has the effect of weakening future resistance.'

'This is absolutely dreadful!' I said. 'Who is making these demands?'

'A few years ago it might well have been our friend Moriarty, who used similar methods on occasions, but at present I have only a suspicion. For that reason I have set the Baker Street Irregulars on to the case. At present, two of them are watching a bakery. I have reason to believe that the baker in question has been propositioned. Hence Tommy's message about the bars.'

'You mean this baker has decided to resist?' I asked.

'It appears so,' he said, 'and our present errand is to see if he will give me any indication of whence came the threat.'

He glanced around him then rapped with his stick on the cab's roof, telling our cabby to halt.

'Let us alight here,' he said. 'I do not wish to draw attention to our arrival at the premises.'

We stepped down from our cab at a busy street crossing and I followed Holmes as he took the left-hand turning from the junction.

We had turned into a commercial street of small shops. It being now late morning there was a steady rattle and clatter of vehicles along the way, mostly tradesmen's vans and carts. The pavements too were busy, with numbers of people going about their shopping. Ahead of us I heard the cheerful melody of a barrel organ and saw a stocky individual in a grubby duster and battered straw hat winding his contrivance at the kerbside.

We had not gone many paces when the barrel organ's melody ended in a sudden, dismal slur. I was wondering what had stopped his cheerful tune when I heard an unearthly shrieking sound from the opposite side of the street, followed by a loud clatter and the cries of bystanders.

'Come, Watson!' commanded Holmes. 'We are, I fear, too late!'

He sprang away across the street and I was about to follow him when a hand plucked at my sleeve.

'Doctor Watson! Doctor Watson!' said the voice of a small boy, who was urgently grasping at my elbow. 'Freddy's ill. You gotta 'elp him!'

Three

A Medical Emergency

My instinct was, as ever, to follow Holmes, but the promptings of the ragamuffin at my side confused me. From across the street the dreadful shrieking sound continued, though I could not recognize the source. Holmes, I saw, was thrusting his way through the crowd that had gathered as crowds always gather when untoward events occur in public.

A glance at the tear-stained and desperate features of the boy who had importuned me, and the recognition that he was the same Tommy whose cryptic message had brought Holmes and me to this spot, convinced me that I must deal with the nearer emergency.

'Where?' I demanded.

He sprang away, running ahead of me along the pavement to where a large horse trough stood almost opposite the scene of the disturbance. As I caught up with him I saw that another lad lay in the shadow of the trough, his tousled head in the gutter. He was clutching his abdomen with both hands and emitting piteous cries in between attempts to vomit into the drain below the trough.

Swiftly I knelt at the boy's side and it took only a glance to diagnose that the lad had been poisoned in some way.

'What have you eaten?' I asked him.

'Nothin',' he gasped. 'Only a bit of an apple, honest!'

I looked about me and spied a small cafeteria. Leaving the sick boy in the care of his friend I dashed in and persuaded the proprietor to supply me with a large jug of heavily salted water. I was back in moments and, with his friend's assistance, succeeded in forcing a large quantity of the saline solution down the afflicted boy's throat.

My crude remedy did its work in minutes and the lad was soon vomiting vigorously into the gutter.

When I judged that the contents of his stomach had been completely discharged, I helped him to his feet and he rinsed his face at the horse trough, scrubbing it dry with the tails of his neckerchief.

I glanced across the street, but the crowd there had enlarged and I could not see Holmes anywhere, so I led the two boys into the little cafeteria and sat them down.

'You,' I said to Freddy, 'are to have nothing but warm milk. Your stomach, indeed your entire system, has had a severe shock, and we must not overburden it.' Once milk was provided, with tea for me and a large Chelsea bun for Tommy, I sought to discover how Freddy had come to be poisoned.

'We was sent by Mr Holmes,' explained Tommy. 'To keep an eye on the baker across the street. Mr Holmes said as we was to let him know if there was bars put up to the window. We been watchin' 'ere three days and this mornin' we seed a couple of fellows puttin' bars to the window, so we let Mr Holmes know by way of a billy doo.'

I doubted whether he had any more understanding of the real meaning of the words than he had of their pronunciation, but I took him to refer to his note to Holmes. I nodded.

'That was what brought Mr Holmes and me,' I said.

'Well,' continued Tommy, 'just before you and Mr Holmes got here, there was a cartload of flour pulled up by the baker's. The carter went inside the shop and we went across to have a look at the 'orses. We was over there, strokin' them and that, when the carter come out the shop and moved us on, a bit rude like, so we come back across 'ere to the waterin' trough.'

Freddy looked up with a milky moustache painted on his grubby features and nodded. 'That was when the foreign cove come along,' he said.

'That's right,' agreed his friend. 'A bloke came along the street with a paper bag. He stood by us and he takes an apple out of the bag and starts eatin' it. After a bit he says to us, "Look at them poor ol' 'orses. I expect they'd like a bite of an apple, don't you?" and he takes out his pocket knife and cuts an apple in two bits. He gives Freddy the bits and says, "Here, take them across to the 'orses, and here's a penny for yourselves."'

'So I took his apple,' said Freddy, 'and went across the street, and on the way I 'ad a bite of it. Well the first bite wasn't half bad. I bit off a bit more, then I give 'alf to each of the 'orses on the flour wagon. I didn't hang about, 'cos the carter had chased us off before. I just come straight back across to where Tommy was. I sits down by the trough and I was still chewin' a bit of the apple, but it tasted nasty, so I spit it out. A little bit after that I got the most unholy pain in the belly.'

'He was hollerin' blue murder,' interjected Tommy. 'I thought as he was larkin' about at first, but I seen his face was sweatin' and he was really cryin' out. I didn't know what to do, then I saw you and Mr Holmes drop down from your cab at the corner and I run for you.'

'I fought as I was dying, Doctor,' Freddy said. 'It was as though me guts was all burnin' up and I wanted to be sick but I couldn't.'

'You might well have died, Freddy,' I told him. 'I suspect you took in a very violent poison, most probably from the apple. How do you feel now?'

'Very much better, Doctor, thanks to you.' He cast his eyes around the room and they came to rest on a glass case filled with cakes on the counter. 'I feel so much better I think I might be able to eat a little,' he hazarded.

'I'm pleased to hear it,' I said, 'but we must not, as I remarked earlier, overstrain your system. I think more milk and a little buttered toast might be in order.'

I had arranged for further refreshments all round when the little bell above the café's door tinkled and Holmes looked in.

'Ah! There you are, Watson, and the Irregulars too, I'll be bound. What has kept you three away from the scene of the crime?'

'Crime?' I said, as Holmes pulled up a chair and joined our table. 'Has there been a crime?'

'There has been,' he said, 'one of those bizarre incidents which are a part of this affair and which, in this case, cannot have been other than a crime.'

We all looked at him expectantly. He gave his order for a pot of tea to the lady at the counter then turned back to us.

'You will recall,' he began, 'that when we left our cab, there was a wagon parked outside the baker's across the street?'

We all nodded and he went on. 'As you and I approached, the horses, each in turn, emitted those fearful shrieks which we heard and went into convulsions, throwing themselves about so vigorously as to upset the wagon and spill much of its load. By the time I arrived, that had occurred and the wretched animals were still writhing and twitching while giving vent to those appalling cries of distress. It was evident that they were not ill in any ordinary sense, for their owner would have seen the signs and not worked them. I formed the view that they had been poisoned, a view which was confirmed when, within minutes of my arrival on the scene, both of the poor creatures fell dead.'

'Poison again,' I remarked.

Holmes seized on my remark. 'Again?' he queried, raising one eyebrow.

I started to explain to him how it was that he found me with the Irregulars in the café, but Tommy and Freddy had been itching to report to Holmes ever since he joined us and rapidly took over my narrative.

Holmes heard them out patiently, interjecting only an occasional question. When they were done he said, 'And can you describe the man with the apples to me?'

They both joined in and, by fits and starts, he extracted a description of a swarthy man in his early thirties, with dark

18

hair, black eyes and a thick moustache, probably more than five and a half feet tall.

'He had shoulders on him,' commented Tommy. 'They stretched his jacket. I thought he was a labourin' man, and his hands was big and rough like a labourer's.'

'Well done,' said Holmes. 'And how was he dressed?'

'Corduroys, a brown velveteen jacket as had seen better days, though it had fancy buttons, and a dark-brown weskit,' recited Freddy.

'And a sort of squashy soft felt hat wiv a jay's feather in the band and a red diklo,' added Tommy.

'Excellent!' exclaimed my friend. 'Do you recall how he spoke?'

'Sorta foreign,' said Tommy and his friend nodded agreement, adding, 'I thought he was a gypsy when I sees the red round his neck, but his voice was foreign, most like an Eye-talian. There's a lot of Eye-talians about here.'

Holmes nodded. 'So now,' he said, 'we know why the horses were poisoned, how and by whom. It remains only to establish the identities of our friend with the apples and the person who issued his orders.'

'Why were the horses poisoned, Holmes?' I asked, for I had not understood this at all.

'Watson! Watson!' he scolded. 'I have explained that this is a matter of insurance. Mr Morelli, the baker, was approached and offered the gang's protection in return for the customary tithe on his profits. He refused and installed iron bars at his premises to prevent any attack on them. He has, despite his precautions, been attacked. A cartload of flour lies scattered in the gutter across the street, two valuable horses are dead, and Mr Morelli is going to have difficulty obtaining supplies. No miller will be anxious to deliver to a bakery where carts and horses are destroyed in broad daylight.'

'What will you do next?' I enquired.

'It is important that I speak to the barrel-organist as soon as possible,' he replied.

'The organ-grinder!' I exclaimed. 'But surely, he had nothing to do with it?'

'Cast your mind back,' said Holmes, 'to the moment when you and I alighted from our cab, and recall the sequence of events as we made our way along the street.'

I thought for a moment. 'You paid off the cabby,' I began, 'while I waited at the kerbside. Then I turned and we walked side by side in this direction along this side of the street.'

'What could you see?' demanded Holmes.

'Why, people going about their business on both sides of the street, carts and vans coming and going, the cart standing outside the baker's, the lads here by the watering trough ahead of us, the organ-grinder up on the next corner. Nothing untoward,' I finished.

He nodded. 'And what did you hear?'

'People chatting as they passed by, cart wheels, hooves, the rattle of harness, the organ-grinder playing. I remember thinking what a jaunty little tune it was and trying to place it.'

'And what first made you aware that something unusual had occurred?' he pressed.

'Well, the cry of the horses. It was a dreadful sound. I've never heard anything quite like it.'

He stared at me. 'You have placed things in the order which you believe is correct,' he said, sternly, 'not the sequence in which they occurred.'

I thought hard. 'Great Heavens!' I said, after a minute or so. 'You're right! The music stopped suddenly, in the middle of the tune. I was wondering why when I heard the noise of the horses and then you called to me. That was the way that things went.'

He sat back in his chair. 'Precisely, Watson. With a little encouragement you make an excellent witness.'

'But what does that tell you about the organ-grinder?' I asked, bewildered.

'The barrel-organist,' he said, 'from his vantage point on the corner of Lantern Street, could see our presumed Italian approach Tommy and Freddy. He will have seen Freddy

20

cross the street with an apple and give a half to each of the horses. A perfectly innocuous scene, one might imagine, which attracted the attention of no one else on the street, yet the barrel-organist ended his music abruptly and made off up Lantern Street.'

'But why?' I said.

'Because, Watson, he was on that corner expecting something to happen at Morelli's bakery. When he saw the transaction between the boys and the man with the apples, he knew that whatever he expected was about to occur, so he made himself scarce. That is why I wish to speak to him. I would very much like to know how he knew what to expect.'

Four

The Contents of a Tea Chest

O ur two Irregulars were eager to seek out the organ-grinder for Holmes and were so commissioned, after which my friend and I made our way back to Baker Street.

'Did you succeed in obtaining any information from the baker?' I asked him on the way.

He shook his head. 'I had information that Mr Morelli had said he would resist any attempts to make him pay the protection levy,' he said, 'but after this morning's event he was unwilling to say anything. The villains have demonstrated their power to harm him and I fear he will now join the ranks of their subscribers.'

'And what steps will you take now?' I enquired.

'I shall wait to see what our organ-grinder can tell us when we meet.'

'You believe that the Irregulars will find him, then?'

'I have every faith in them, Watson,' he said and changed the subject.

On the following morning Holmes and I had completed our breakfast when Mrs Hudson told us that Inspector Lestrade had arrived.

When he was shown in, the little detective refused Holmes' offer of the basket chair. 'I'm on my way to look at a body,' he explained. 'It has been found on some wasteland off Biskett Street and no one seems to know how he died. The local Division thinks it may well be murder.'

To mention a mysterious cadaver to Sherlock Holmes is akin to dangling a fat and juicy fly in front of a Hampshire trout. Within minutes we were in the street, clambering into the four-wheeler which had brought Lestrade.

'Now,' said Holmes, as our cabby headed his horses out of Baker Street, 'tell us what you can of this mysterious corpse, Lestrade.'

'Well, I only know what the local Division have telephoned to the Yard, Mr Holmes, which isn't much, but it seems it was found by a couple of young lads who were scouting the wasteland for rubbish. You know people will throw their rubbish away in these places and sometimes there's bits and pieces that can be used or sold.'

'Yes, yes,' said my friend impatiently. 'Two boys found the body. How was it lying?'

'Well, as I understand it, it wasn't lying at all. It was in a box.'

'In a box!' I exclaimed.

'Well, a tea chest, I think,' said Lestrade.

'Has the man been identified?' asked Holmes.

'Not so far as I know,' admitted Lestrade. 'It seems he has no clothes on, but no one can tell how he was killed.'

'You seem to have very few facts, Lestrade,' Holmes remarked sharply. 'Where is the body now?'

'I know that, Mr Holmes. It's at the Divisional Station. I told them to hold on to it until we arrived.'

'Then, since you can tell us nothing, it seems I shall have to contain myself until we arrive there,' snapped Holmes and fell silent, drumming his fingers on the head of his stick and staring out of the window until we stopped.

We drew up at last alongside a patch of weed-strewn wasteland, a gap in the array of shops and houses where two sizeable shops had been pulled down. The rank growth of weeds was high, partially concealing the chunks of rubble and brickwork that lay about the site, and the domestic refuse, from mattresses to cast-iron baths, which had found a home there.

'I thought you would wish to see where the tea chest was found, Mr Holmes,' said Lestrade, leading us through the weeds for a few paces. 'It was here,' he said, pointing to a small area of crushed vegetation.

Holmes plucked a sprig from a sprouting weed and sniffed it. 'Hmm,' he said. 'Your tea chest was placed here no earlier than last night. Had yesterday's sun shone on these broken plants they would have dried by now, but the sap is relatively fresh.' He stared about him, stooping once or twice to examine the ground around us.

'I see nothing else of any consequence here, Lestrade,' he said. 'Your colleagues have thoroughly trampled the area in removing the corpse and it is impossible to distinguish any earlier prints. Let us view the body.'

We regained our vehicle and travelled through a couple of streets before turning into the yard of the Divisional Police Headquarters.

Lestrade led us to a shed, where a large tea chest stood on a trestle table.

'The body has not, I take it, been unpacked?' remarked Holmes, as a uniformed Inspector and a sergeant joined us.

'No, sir,' said the Inspector. 'When discovered, the corpse was in a state of total rigor. To remove it from the chest would have involved smashing the chest and possibly breaking the cadaver's limbs. I thought it best to await the normal passage of the rigor mortis, sir.'

'Quite right, Inspector,' approved Holmes. 'Has it yet passed off?' and he leaned over the chest and poked the contents with an experimental finger.

'I think so, sir,' said the Inspector, and Holmes nodded agreement. 'So, we can reasonably infer that he died some twelve hours ago, eh, Watson?'

'Possibly,' I agreed, 'though one cannot be sure. Sometimes rigor mortis does not even occur. It is only a rough guide.'

Holmes stood and pondered a moment, stroking his chin with the fingers of one hand.

'I think it will be best', he said at last, 'if we try to remove him from the tea chest without damaging it. We do not know what it may yet tell us.'

All five of us surrounded the box and began, with great care, the complicated task of removing the cadaver from its casing. The body seemed to be in a kneeling position, with its arms hung down in front of it and its head pushed under the rim of the tea chest. Once we had worked the head and shoulders free it became relatively easy to lift it from the box and lay it along the trestle.

'I wonder, Watson,' said Holmes, once the dead man was laid out, 'if you would be so good as to examine our friend here while I see what I can make of his erstwhile container.'

The corpse was that of a clean-shaven man of about thirty, some five feet and eight inches tall, with thick black hair and black eyes. His musculature suggested that he had been a labouring man, and a darkish complexion suggested foreign blood. Here and there about his person there were abrasions, apparently from connection with the tea chest and equally apparently inflicted after death, inasmuch as they had not bled.

What concerned me was the absence of any indication as to how he had died. That he was not strangled I could determine by the absence of any ligature mark about the neck or petechiae around the eyes, but I could find no indication of any other kind of assault, nor of any wounds to the hands or arms that might have indicated an attempt to defend himself.

I turned at last to Holmes, who was painstakingly taking the tea chest apart with his pocket knife. 'Holmes,' I said. 'I am at a loss to determine the cause of death here. He seems to have been a healthy man, or at least, I can see no signs of disease, but I can see no signs of violence. If he was murdered, I can only suggest that it was by some poisonous agent that shows no external traces.'

'With all respect to your expertise, Watson, I should doubt

that,' he said. Laying down a section of the tea chest, he pocketed his knife and took out his mechanical pencil. 'I suggest you recall the death of Edward II.'

I did not catch his reference for a moment, then light dawned. 'But Edward II,' I protested, 'was killed by a red-hot poker inserted in his—'

'Precisely, Watson,' he interrupted. 'Do you, by any chance, have a white handkerchief?'

I passed him one, wondering what use he proposed to make of it, and he wound a corner of it carefully around the tip of his mechanical pencil then, to the astonishment of all of us, inserted it carefully into the left ear of the corpse. After turning it around a couple of times he drew it out and held it up triumphantly.

'There!' he exclaimed, and pointed to the blood which now stained the corner of my handkerchief. 'There is your cause of death, Watson. He was killed by a stiletto or some similarly slender implement being driven through the eardrum into the brain.'

'But that is not how Edward II died!' I protested.

'Indeed not,' he agreed. 'He was killed with a red-hot spit inserted through a horn into his anus, but the intention was the same – that the body would show no exterior marks of violence.'

'It is hardly surprising that I missed it,' I grumbled.

'You might have looked for it in the unexplained death of an Italian,' Holmes replied. 'It is a characteristic method of murder which also has the advantage that there is little blood to clean up.'

'An Italian!' I exclaimed. 'How can you possibly tell that?'

'His complexion reveals him to have been darker skinned than the average Briton, while his crucifix and the style of his moustache suggest a Roman Catholic with a characteristically Italian moustache.'

'But he has no crucifix and he is clean-shaven!' I protested.

Holmes stepped towards the body. 'Observe,' he commanded, pointing to the cadaver's upper chest, 'the pale mark where something has hung about his neck for a long time. Do you agree that the mark is cruciform? A crucifix, most probably, strongly suggesting a Roman Catholic.'

'Very well,' I conceded, 'but you must admit that he has no moustache, Holmes.'

'Observe again,' he said. 'His upper lip, though swarthy, is lighter than the rest of his face. In other words, it has not been so long exposed to the sun. The pale area is very much the shape of the moustache normally worn by Italian males and if you borrow my glass I think you will see that there are traces of stubble in that area.'

'But why would he shave off his moustache?' I asked.

Holmes leant over the dead man and applied his lens to the face. 'I did not say that he shaved off his moustache, Watson. Look here,' and he handed me the glass.

'You see,' he went on. 'His cheeks and chin show an even, slight stubble, that indicates a man who shaved cleanly in the morning and whose stubble is reappearing. It might even be possible, if we knew the rate of growth of his beard and the time of his last shave, to determine the time of his death from those factors, but I digress. Across his upper lip the stubble is different. It is less profuse, having been more recently cut, and less cleanly removed. Then there is the direction of the strokes.'

'How can you tell that?' I asked, peering through the lens.

'The irregular fragments of stubble left behind show the direction,' he said. 'You are right-handed, Watson. How would you remove your moustache?'

'Why, by stroking from the centre to the outside on each side of the mouth, I suppose,' I said.

'Precisely,' he agreed. 'But this gentleman's moustache was removed by strokes from above down to the lip, with a slight left to right bias.'

'And what does that mean?'

'It means, Watson, that he was shaved by someone else, a right-handed person who shaved him quickly and clumsily, solely in order to remove the moustache and make identification difficult.'

'He might be a Spanish sailor, dumped after a tavern brawl,' the uniformed Inspector complained.

Holmes lifted one eyebrow. 'So he might,' he agreed. 'But such a victim would have been left in an alley or flung into the river, and his body would bear the clear marks of bludgeon, knife or brass knuckles. In addition to which,' and he pointed, 'Watson has also not mentioned that the ears are pierced to take earrings, a Sicilian fashion, I believe.'

'I see,' I said. 'Is there anything else that I failed to observe?'

'Only this,' he said, and opened the corpse's mouth. He lifted the tongue with one hand and removed something white from beneath it. It was a small piece of paper, folded twice.

Holmes unfolded it and laid it on the edge of the trestle table. All that the paper showed was a grid of four lines, two across two.

'A noughts-and-crosses game!' exclaimed the uniformed Inspector.

'I very much doubt it,' observed Holmes. 'I have known cards lead to fatalities, and horse racing and even football, but I believe that noughts and crosses is a relatively safe pastime. This is the marker of an organization that rejoices in the name "The Rule of Nine". I was not previously aware of their existence in London.'

'But who are they?' asked Lestrade.

Five

A Pause For Tea

'The Rule of Nine,' said Holmes, 'is one of the Italian secret societies, similar to the Black Hand Gang, and like them is ordinarily rooted in the Lower East Side of New York. If they have come to London, then you will have your work cut out for you, Lestrade.'

The two Inspectors' faces grew more and more thoughtful as my friend outlined to them his theories as to the operations of a protection gang and the events of the previous day.

'But what do you say this fellow has to do with all that?' asked Lestrade, indicating the corpse.

'He seems,' said Holmes, 'to be the man who poisoned the horses yesterday. He has been executed by his superiors for some offence and his body left in public, so that those who knew nothing would remain in ignorance, but those who knew the gang would understand that the Rule of Nine had exacted its penalty.'

'But why would they penalize him?' I asked. 'He seems to have carried out his orders.'

'So he did, Watson, but they will blame him for drawing my attention to the matter.'

He suggested to Lestrade that a portrait of the dead man with a moustache added should be circulated for identification purposes, and we left.

I admit that I was silent as we took a cab. I still felt that Holmes had misled me by his reference to Edward II and that he could hardly expect me to carry in my memory the characteristic modes of killing of all nations and peoples.

When at last I recovered my humour and ventured a remark it was to ask, 'Did you find anything in the tea chest, Holmes?'

'Certainly,' he said. 'Tea,' and with that he changed the subject.

I had taken no notice of our journey and was startled when my friend rapped on the roof to halt the cabby. As we stepped down I looked about and was unable to recognize our whereabouts, though I noted a strong smell of fresh coffee on the air.

Holmes saw my puzzlement and pointed his stick at a sign hanging over the pavement. It read, 'Greenfrew and Massley, Tea Importers and Blenders.'

'We need,' said Holmes, 'the services of an expert, and where else are they to be found but in Mincing Lane?'

I followed him through the door beneath the sign and found myself in a small shop. It was divided across by a plain deal counter, behind which stood two pleasant-seeming young women in plain grey dresses and aprons. At their rear, shelves supported a double row of huge tin canisters, each some three feet tall and cast in the common shape of a cylindrical tea caddy. Painted in bold reds, blues and greens, each can bore on its front a different flag or emblem in full colour and, in gold letters, the name of one of the tea-producing territories whose product, I imagine, was contained within.

Holmes passed his card to the older shop assistant and asked to see Mr Greenfrew. She took the card through a door at the back of the shop and was absent for a few minutes before she returned and invited us to follow her.

At the top of two flights of stairs she showed us into a pleasant chamber whose windows gave a view of rooftops below and the masts of ships on the Thames.

A small, plump gentleman, with gold-rimmed spectacles and thick white hair fringing a bald pate, rose from his chair at the end of a long, polished table and came around the table to meet us, his eyes alight behind his lenses.

'Mr Holmes!' he cried. 'What a pleasure! What a pleasure! And this will be your amanuensis whose acquaintance has not previously been vouchsafed me. I have followed your accounts of Mr Holmes' doings with great interest,' he assured me and shook my hand vigorously.

Once we were seated beside his table he eyed us thoughtfully. 'An Earl Grey for you, Mr Holmes, I think, but something more robust, perhaps an Assam, for your colleague. Yes, an Earl Grey and an Assam for our visitors,' he commanded his shop assistant, who had waited at the door.

'Now then,' he said, turning back to us. 'What little puzzle have you brought me today, Mr Holmes?'

My friend reached into his coat pocket and produced a screw of white paper, passing it to our host.

The little man's eyes lit up again as he laid the paper carefully on the table and peered at it from all directions. At last he looked up at Holmes. 'An unknown blend?' he asked. 'For me to identify?' And his enthusiasm was childlike.

Holmes smiled. 'As you surmise,' he said. 'An unknown blend. I have always been assured that there is no finer nor more perceptive nose or palate in Britain when it comes to tea, Mr Greenfrew. I shall be grateful for anything you are able to tell me about this blend.'

'If it was blended in Britain then I have tasted it,' declared Greenfrew and carefully unfolded the paper, revealing a small mound of what seemed to me to be a very ordinary tea, then peered at it closely, sniffing as he did so. He kept this up for some minutes while a tap at the door heralded his shop assistant with two small pots of tea for Holmes and me.

Our host looked up. 'It is fairly coarse blend,' he said, 'but one that I think I should recognize. There is enough here for a small infusion. Let me make one up while you take your refreshment, gentlemen.'

Quickly he poured out cups for my friend and me, then went to a cabinet at the back of the room and produced a spirit burner, kettle and teapot. Once he had lit the burner and placed the kettle he returned to the table.

'What do you make of our new Earl Grey?' he asked Holmes.

Holmes turned the tea in his mouth. 'It is fruitier and more refreshing than I am used to,' he said and Greenfrew smiled. 'There is, I think, more than an ordinary Earl Grey blend here. There is a trace of lime and something else.'

'Ah, Mr Holmes,' Greenfrew said, 'you are very perceptive. I have added a touch of a third leaf and a smidgen of lime.' He shook his bald head. 'What a palate you might have had if you were not a smoker. Have you never thought of abandoning tobacco?'

Holmes smiled. 'Never,' he said. 'Watson will tell you that there are many occasions when tobacco is my only assistant in finding my way through a complicated enquiry. I take it you have never smoked?'

'Absolutely not!' exclaimed Greenfrew. 'My sense of taste is so valuable to me that I have recently had to remove from the front of this building to the rear. Since those confounded coffee merchants set up business nearby the whole street stinks of their roasting beans and the stench was pervading my rooms and making it impossible for me to distinguish among the lighter varieties of tea. Even now, when the wind off the river is in the wrong quarter, I have to close the shutters in order to protect my nose and palate.'

His kettle boiled and he set about making a pot from Holmes' specimen. When he had done he brought it to the table with a cup and poured himself a little, sniffing the steam that rose from the cup. I confess that my own enjoyment of my tea was blunted by my recollection of Holmes scraping his sample from the crevices of the chest which had carried the corpse.

'Let it brew a little,' he said, 'as this kind of tea is intended. Now, Doctor, how do you like your Assam?'

'Very well,' I said. 'It is a robust and tasteful drink, which I would imagine to have excellent restorative powers.'

'Oh, it has, it has,' he said. 'I am glad to see you take only a little milk, Doctor. People are so inclined to swamp the tea with milk. I have even seen people add cream to it, would you believe? And, worse yet, some people have contracted the French habit of putting the milk in first. Once you do that the flavour of the tea is lost, lost completely.'

'Have you been in India?' I enquired.

He shook his head. 'It is my eternal regret that I have never visited any of the lands which bear tea plants.'

'When I was there,' I said, 'I saw the natives boiling tea in milk with spices. That's a pretty unusual brew, I can tell you.'

He made an expression of disgust and turned to the sample which he had poured for himself.

'Yes,' he mused, 'a coarse blend of two Indian leaves.' He took a sip and swilled it in his mouth, eventually spitting it out into a fingerbowl.

'Do you wish to know from what leaves it is blended?' he asked Holmes.

'Not unless it is material. I am more interested in the firm that created it and where it might be sold.'

'Oh, the firm that created it is easy,' said Greenfrew. 'This is one of a number of coarse breakfast blends created by Staunton and Miller. I must say that it is more coarse than I would wish as a start to the day.'

'And where would I find it sold?' asked Holmes.

'Very widely,' said the little man. 'Very widely. I do not think you can limit the scope of your enquiries from this. Staunton's Breakfast Teas are a staple of cheap grocery purveyors all over London and the surrounding counties. Have you no other information?'

'The sample came from the interior of a used tea chest,' said Holmes. 'The letters M and E with a stroke between were chalked on the outside of the chest, though there is no means of knowing how long they had been there.'

Greenfrew took another sip from his cup and repeated his tasting routine. 'This specimen is very fresh,' he said. 'These cheap, coarse teas lose their flavour rapidly, but this seems to be at about full strength. The letters M and E would indicate that it was part of a consignment for Morris Evans, the grocers. They have, however, branches all over London. All I can tell you is that Stauntons blended this recently and shipped it to a branch of Morris Evans.'

'Do Staunton and Miller have premises here?' asked Holmes.

'Oh no,' said Greenfrew. 'We superior blenders like to be near the docks, but Stauntons buy whatever is left over when we have taken our pick. You'll find their warehouse at the north end of Lantern Street.'

'Lantern Street,' repeated Holmes. 'Thank you, Mr Greenfrew. I think you have assisted in pointing us in the right direction.'

As we left the premises I could not resist asking Holmes, 'Why did you not tell him the exact circumstances in which you accumulated that specimen of tea, Holmes?'

He looked at me blankly. 'Do you imagine,' he said, 'that it would have assisted his discrimination, Watson, to know that he was drinking tea that had shared its chest with a corpse?'

We had arrived back in Baker Street and left our cab when we were surrounded by a gaggle of young ragamuffins. It was, of course, the Irregulars, come to report to their chief.

'We found 'im, Mr Holmes!' one cried. 'We went and 'ung about the warehouse where they 'ires their organs, and we got 'im. 'E's called "Parsley" or somefink like that an' he lives back of Lantern Lane, in an Eye-talian boarding house.'

Holmes thanked them, noted their information in his pocketbook and paid them handsomely, so that they went whooping away towards the Marylebone Road, scattering passers-by as they went.

As we turned back to the street, in search of a cab, a four-wheeler drew up alongside us and Inspector Lestrade's sallow face appeared at the window.

'The very men!' he exclaimed. 'You may berate the official police, Mr Holmes, but we are before you this time. I'm on my way to visit this here organ-grinder and I thought you might wish to accompany me.'

'Indeed,' said Holmes, affably. 'Watson and I were just about to set out for Mrs Ruggiero's at the back of Lantern Lane, but I dare say your cab is as good as another.'

I saw the little detective's face fall as we climbed into the conveyance.

Six

A Taste of Parsley

Mrs Ruggiero's establishment turned out to be a forbidding, red-brick building of four storeys, with small but gaily curtained windows breaking its dark frontage. We drove to it along a narrow street of similar houses, where bright-eyed, dark-skinned children, clothed mostly in tatters, played across the street and only avoided our wheels and hooves at the last moment.

As we stood on the front doorstep Lestrade knocked vigorously.

The door was answered by a plump, swarthy woman of about sixty, dressed all in black apart from a white apron, on which she was wiping her hands. She stood silently in the open doorway and awaited our introduction.

Lestrade touched his hat. 'Good day, madam,' he said. 'Would you be Mrs Ruggiero?'

She eyed him suspiciously before replying. At last she said, '*Si*, that is my name. What you want?'

The Inspector smiled. 'I was wondering whether you had a lodger here who operates a barrel organ? An organ-grinder?'

'I got three lodgers who work barrel organs,' she said. 'What name you want?'

Lestrade looked flustered, but Holmes cut in. 'The name might be "Parsley",' he suggested.

She looked nonplussed. 'Parsley, Parsley,' she repeated, 'is not a name. Is plant you put in cooking. I got no one name of Parsley here. You make joke of me.'

She turned, about to close the door on us, but paused. She swung back and a light dawned in her face.

'You mean Par–sell–i,' she said, emphasizing each syllable. 'I gotta organ-grinder called Parselli. You want him?'

'Certainly,' said Holmes. 'It will be Mr Parselli that we wish to see.'

She turned her back on us again with a curt, 'You wait here,' and closed the door on us.

Two or three minutes later the door reopened. This time we were confronted by a short, stocky, dark man, with round, black eyes and a small moustache. He was only a little over five feet tall and his brown features were lightly pockmarked. He wore a red waistcoat over a collarless striped shirt and velveteen trousers which flared at the lower ends, and his waistcoat was ornamented by a cheap and decorative American watch on a chain. He looked sullenly around our small group.

'What you want?' he demanded suddenly, and the Italian accent was obvious.

'We were looking for a Mr Par–sell–i,' said Lestrade, emphasizing the syllables as the landlady had done.

'I am Parselli,' said the man. 'What you want?'

'You operate a barrel organ, I believe?' said Lestrade.

The man cast his eyes heavenward, then stared at Lestrade. 'You ask Mrs Ruggiero for an organ-grinder. You know fine I operate an organ. What you want, Mister?'

'Inspector,' Lestrade corrected him. 'Metropolitan Police. Do you own the organ you use?'

The man stepped out on to the pavement and pointed upwards.

'You see,' he said, 'that little window up under the roof. Is my room, where I live. You think I keep a barrel organ up there, Mister Policeman? You think I wheel it upstairs every night and downstairs every morning, eh? I hire an organ daily from Benetti's warehouse, like all the other organ-grinders.'

'There's no call for impertinence,' said Lestrade, huffily. 'Have you got a Metropolitan Police licence?'

The Italian put a thumb and forefinger into his waistcoat pocket and produced a folded paper, which he handed to Lestrade.

Lestrade looked over the document and retained it. 'Suppose I say that I'm not satisfied with this licence?' he asked. 'Suppose I say that I want to know what you know?'

'What I know about what?' said the organ-grinder, and his tone was now positively belligerent.

Lestrade smiled. 'Well, perhaps we might say the two carthorses that were poisoned outside Morelli's, the baker, the other day. You know about that, don't you?'

The organ-grinder's right fist struck Lestrade in the face before any of us could intervene, knocking the little detective to the ground. The attacker sprang forward, apparently to escape, but I was ready for him by that time and swung my stick between his ankles, causing him to stumble and fall.

As the Italian scrambled up from the pavement, Holmes took hold of him firmly, while I helped Lestrade to his feet. His sallow face was white and working with rage.

'Right, my lad!' he snarled at our prisoner. 'You've done it now. You've assaulted an officer of the Metropolitan Police in the execution of his duty and I am now arresting you for the said assault.'

Holmes had been smiling inscrutably throughout the exchange between Parselli and Lestrade, and was still doing so.

'Hold hard, Lestrade!' he said. 'Arresting this gentleman might be a serious error.'

'Error be damned!' said Lestrade. 'Not arrest a foreign hurdy-gurdy grinder that's laid his hands on an Inspector of Police, Mr Holmes? I'd be failing in my duty!'

'Nevertheless,' said Holmes. 'There is something here that you should consider.'

Maintaining a firm grip on his prisoner, Holmes slid his fingers inside the Italian's waistcoat, producing a small leather case. He flipped it open, showing us that it contained a shield-shaped metal badge with some kind of inscription, then closed it and returned it to Parselli's inside pocket.

'Let me effect a proper introduction,' he said, smiling broadly now. 'Inspector Lestrade, permit me to introduce Detective Joseph Petrosino of the New York Police Department.'

'A Yankee copper! Well, I'm blowed!' exclaimed Lestrade. 'What are you doing on my patch, making out like an organ-grinder?'

'I will tell you that, Inspector, when you have arrested me. I apologize for striking you, but I must be seen to be arrested.'

'With pleasure!' Lestrade declared, and reaching into his pocket he produced a pair of handcuffs and fixed them on the organ-grinder's wrists. Holmes meanwhile was rapping on the front door with his stick.

In a moment Mrs Ruggiero reappeared, muttering in Italian. 'What you want now?' she demanded.

'Perhaps you will be kind enough to bring Mr Parselli's hat and coat,' said Holmes, smiling affably. 'It has proved necessary to arrest him.'

The landlady cast her eyes upward and invoked several saints in Italian, but went back in without any further comment, returning in minutes with her lodger's coat and a wide-brimmed felt hat. Lestrade had kept our four-wheeler and now beckoned it to pick us up. Soon we were all settled inside it.

'Now,' said Sherlock Holmes, once we were well under way, 'I think we should make for Baker Street, rather than any police station, and while we are on the way, perhaps Officer Petrosino will tell us what a New York Detective is doing masquerading as an organ-grinder and living in a London lodging house which is approved by the Rule of Nine.'

Petrosino's eyes widened and he stared at Holmes. 'You know that?' he said. 'How do you know that?'

'Because I noted their four-line symbol chalked on the left-hand doorpost,' said Holmes. 'I imagine that is what took you to Mrs Ruggiero's premises.'

Petrosino nodded. 'It is,' he said. 'But who are you? You are not a police detective, I think.'

'My name is Sherlock Holmes, and this is my friend and colleague, Dr Watson.'

The American detective stared for a moment. 'But how did you know my name, Mr Holmes?'

'I was told that a certain barrel-organist in whom I was interested was lodging at Mrs Ruggiero's and that his name was "Parsley". As soon as I saw you I recalled items in the American press about an Italian detective in New York who has just been appointed by Commissioner Roosevelt to take charge of serious Italian crimes in the city. Not only did the description match, but I was aware that New Yorkers had nicknamed him "Parsley" because that is what his name means. I am ever scornful of coincidence and, when you deliberately provoked poor Lestrade here, I was quite certain that you were living under cover in that house and needed to be arrested in order to maintain your false identity.'

Petrosino shook his head slowly from side to side. 'Remarkable,' he said. 'I have heard of you, too, Mr Holmes, but I did not believe what I read.'

'Much that has been published about me is fiction,' agreed Holmes. 'Even the accounts by Watson here have a distressing tendency to concentrate on the dramatic or the bizarre aspects of my cases, ignoring my deductive methods. I imagine that the newspaper accounts of your own cases are similarly distorted?'

The American nodded.

'Nevertheless,' Holmes continued, 'I formed the impression that you had succeeded where others had failed or had not, indeed, tried, to suppress the Italian secret societies.'

'I wish it could be said that I have succeeded,' said Petrosino, glumly. 'I have achieved some success, but they flourish like fireweed in the Lower East Side. When I first joined the force the Department had no one who even spoke Italian. They found a corpse one day and the Lieutenant in the case put it down as a ritual murder because the dead man wore a medallion of a man nailed to a cross! But then, he was Jewish and knew nothing of Catholic practice.'

We laughed, and Holmes suggested that Lestrade might like to remove the American's handcuffs.

'Of course!' exclaimed Lestrade, as though he had forgotten, and freed our guest.

Holmes looked out of the window. 'Here we are at Baker Street,' he announced. 'Now we can hear our friend's story in comfort.'

Seven

The Rule of Nine

Within minutes we were settled in our sitting room, Petrosino occupying the basket chair, while Holmes passed around drinks and cigars. When he had served us all, Holmes dropped into a chair opposite the American.

'So,' he said, 'you are in London on the trail of the Rule of Nine, Detective?'

Lestrade interrupted. 'I understand that this Rule of Nine is a secret criminal society,' he said, 'but why is it so called?'

'These people,' said Petrosino, 'are criminals from the old country, from Italy and Sicily. There is a long tradition there of kidnapping and extortion in the name of gangs with fancy names. In America they see much more money and they enlarge their methods, but each little group of them invents a melodramatic name – they call themselves the Black Hand or the Rule of Nine or what you like, to frighten people. I know of at least five gangs which claim to be the Black Hand.'

'How about the Mafia?' I asked.

'The Mafia!' he snorted. 'All these little associations of bandits claim that they are the Mafia. They say it is an ancient patriotic society from Sicily, formed to oppose the French, but it is just another bunch of thieves, murderers and extortionists, like the Rule of Nine.'

He paused. 'All of them,' he went on, 'have complicated rigmaroles of initiation and membership, to keep their members in fear. The Rule of Nine is called so because it has nine rules of membership to which all of its members swear obedience.'

He lifted his head, closed his eyes and began to recite from memory: 'Rule One – any member who reveals to an outsider any operations of his companions, or offends or quarrels with a fellow member, or refuses or fails to comply with an order, or who leaves town for more than a day without notice, shall be fined twenty dollars and cannot come to his place, but the members who judge him must be all of one mind, for or against . . .'

'What does "come to his place" mean?' asked Holmes.

'It means that he cannot take his place at their secret meetings,' said Petrosino, and went on: 'Rule Two – he who swears falsely, or who draws a weapon on a companion who has not a weapon of the same dimension, with the point uncovered if it is a knife, or who fights a duel with another member of the Society, shall be deprived of his rights.

'Rule Three – any companion who knows of a fault committed by another member and does not inform the Society is liable to the same penalty.

'Rule Four – he that does not attend at the precise hour a meeting of the blackmailers of the day, to do his duty, shall be punished. If he has a satisfactory explanation for his lateness he will be pardoned and may take his place, otherwise he shall not participate in the next division of profits.

'Rule Five – a member who produces profit to the Society is entitled to one-fifth as his own share.

'Rule Six – the Society shall not act without the agreement of all companions. The opposition of even one mouth is enough to overrule the opinions of all the others, providing that the person objecting can give a reasonable explanation of his objections.

'Rule Seven – no companion who becomes a member of the Society may in any way alter its Nine Rules.

'Rule Eight – every meeting of the Society must be announced to those on duty on the day of the meeting at least twenty-four hours before it takes place, except in emergencies.

'Rule Nine – the date and place of meetings is entirely

in the hands of the Head of the Society and none may oppose him.'

He opened his eyes. 'Those are the Nine Rules,' he said. 'All of the gangs have something very similar. They also have a tenth rule, which is so well understood that it does not need to be written out. It is called *omertà*.'

'*Omertà?*' queried Lestrade.

'*Omertà*,' the American repeated. 'The rule of silence. The rule that governs their members absolutely, because they exact fearful punishments on those that they even suspect of informing or speaking carelessly.'

'I must say,' I remarked, 'that it all sounds very well organized.'

'So it is,' said the American. 'And getting better. The network of these gangs is becoming like a huge octopus, strangling New York with its extortion, its protection rackets, its brothels, its boy houses. I am in London because one of the principals of the Rule of Nine is here. He is wanted in New York for murder; he will not go back to Sicily because the authorities there know him. So he comes to London, where he is not known, and here he begins his extortion and protection games on fresh ground. When I hear this, I took leave and came here.'

'So you are here unofficially?' said Lestrade.

Petrosino laughed. 'I do not think Commissioner Roosevelt would approve of my living in London as Sandro Parselli the organ-grinder. He does not much approve of me going into the East Side in disguise.'

'Who is the man you want in London?' asked Holmes.

'Vito Corese,' said the American. 'You know of him?'

Holmes shook his head. 'I thought not,' said Petrosino. 'That is precisely why he is here, because no one here knows of him. In Italy he is known, in America he is wanted, but here he is anonymous.'

'And why do you want him?' asked Holmes.

'He set up a forgery gang in New York, Mr Holmes.'

'I thought,' said Holmes, 'that forgery was investigated

by your Secret Service. Is it not an arm of your Treasury Department?'

Petrosino nodded. 'So it is, but the Secret Service deals with forgery all over the United States, and it does not deal with murder. Murder is not a federal offence. When murder happens in New York, that is my business, not the Secret Service's.'

'And this Corese has killed?' said my friend.

'Many times, Mr Holmes. Not only is he a forger, a blackmailer, an extortionist and a protection racketeer, he kills without a blink of the eye. In New York the Rule of Nine fell out over the disposal of the profits from their forgery and Corese had three of them killed. When I put the pressure on, he disappeared. Now I know he is in London.'

'You make your hunt for Corese sound personal, Detective,' observed Holmes.

'Personal!' the American exclaimed. 'It *is* personal, Mr Holmes. In America, in New York, there are many thousands of us who have come from Italy to make a better life. There are Italians in every trade and profession, even now in the Police Department, all making an honest living and doing our best to prosper and feed our families. All of us are tarred with the filth of these wretched gangsters, who make the word "Italian" stink in the noses of Americans, so that they think we are all thieves and killers. It is wrong, Mr Holmes, and I will not have it so!'

He stopped suddenly and took a long draught from his glass of brandy. Holmes nodded, sympathetically. 'And Corese has come to London because he is unknown here and can operate with impunity,' he said.

'You know it, Mr Holmes. You were at Morelli's bakery when the horses were poisoned. I saw you. You were not there by chance, were you?'

'No,' agreed Holmes, and I saw you, and you were not there by chance, either, were you?'

'No, I was not. I do not know where Corese is hiding, but I know that he has already set up a protection business in London. I believed that Morelli had been propositioned and had refused to pay, so that I knew something would happen. I kept watch, and when I saw one of Corese's men give the little street boys an apple for the horses I knew what was happening. They have done that trick before, in New York.'

'Did you know,' said Holmes, 'that the Rule of Nine have killed the man who poisoned the horses?'

'No,' said Petrosino, 'but it does not surprise me. He failed to carry out his duty discreetly. He drew your attention to what was happening.'

'Do you know who he was?' asked Lestrade.

'He was a minor member of the gang, a Giuseppe Cantoni.'

Lestrade wrote the name in his pocketbook. 'But you don't know where Corese is?' he said.

Petrosino shook his head. 'No, but I must find him soon. Something important is coming to a head in London soon.'

'How do you mean?' asked Holmes.

'Does the name of Cardinal Tosca mean anything to you, Mr Holmes?'

Holmes had been lighting his briar. 'Cardinal Tosca,' he said, cautiously. 'Yes, I have heard of the gentleman.'

'He is in London,' said Petrosino. 'It is only the second time that he has ever been here. He was here seven years ago and now he is here again. Do you know why he is here?'

'I wish that I did,' said Holmes. 'I understand him to be here for private reasons.'

'Exactly!' exclaimed the American. 'For private reasons. Last time he was here as the Holy Father's emissary to receive the Morence Cameos, but they were stolen.'

'They were stolen and Father Grant was murdered,' corrected Holmes.

'Exactly so,' said Petrosino. 'I have reasons to believe that Corese and the Rule of Nine were involved in the theft of the Vatican Cameos and that Cardinal Tosca's appearance in London at the same time as Vito Corese is not a coincidence.'

'Coincidence as an explanation,' observed Holmes, 'is always ready to hand, but rarely fits the case. What can you tell us about Cardinal Tosca?'

'I can tell you a great deal about that man,' said Petrosino.

Holmes had sat with his head bowed over his pipe, holding a matchbox to the bowl to improve the draw. Now he looked up and there was an intense gleam in his eyes.

'Then pray do so, Detective Petrosino, pray do so.'

Eight

The Choirboy

Detective Petrosino lifted his eyes to the ceiling, as he had when reciting the Rule of Nine, then began.

'Salvatore Pietro Tosca,' he said, 'was born into a large, poor family in the hills of Sicily. He was the sixth son of a poor farmer, who had also four daughters. When he was small his parents could not afford to send him to school, so he was sent out with his older brothers to look after his father's goats. He was not very good at this. He would leave his flock and go away from them for hours at a time. When he grew older, when he was expected sometimes to camp out in the hills with his goats, he would disappear also, sometimes being gone for days and nights. It was said that he used to walk into towns and villages at night and carry out robberies, then go back to his flock. His father grew more and more angry with him and at last he threw him out of the house. The word was in his village that he would soon be hanged or shot.'

The Italian paused and looked down thoughtfully at his feet. 'But he was not hanged or shot,' he continued. 'When his father disowned him, he was taken in by the Church. The village priest took him into his own home, letting him live in the priest's house, and he became an altar boy and a servant to the priest. Also he began to sing in the Church and people were astonished that he had a beautiful voice.'

'So, he was rescued from a life of crime,' I remarked.

'So it was said, at the time, *Dottore*,' Petrosino went on, 'but soon there were new stories about the boy. Not only was he a beautiful singer, but he had grown into a very

48

handsome youth, and people started to say that the priest had taken him into his house because there was an unnatural relationship between them. These stories were told far and wide, so that something had to be done for the reputation of the Church.'

'What was done?' asked Holmes.

'His father had died,' said the American, 'and his mother and family would not have him home because of the stories about him—'

'Suggesting,' interrupted Holmes, 'that those closest to him were aware of the truth of the allegations.'

'Most probably,' agreed the American detective. 'But whatever their reason, they would not have him back. So the Bishop stepped in, so as to quiet the scandal. The old priest was sent away from the parish to a foundation in Messina, and the boy was sent to a school in Rome.'

'In Rome!' I exclaimed.

'No less, *Dottore*. The Bishop apparently believed that underneath this singing scugnizzo there was something of value to be rescued. The boy was educated in Rome and afterwards sent to a seminary to study for the priesthood.'

'And did he qualify?' I asked.

'Oh, yes,' said Petrosino. 'In due time he took orders and was sent to a parish in the north of Italy.'

Holmes lifted a hand to stop the Italian. 'By this time,' he said, 'it must have been several years later. Can we take it that no scandal attached to his name while he was studying for the priesthood?'

Petrosino nodded. 'So far as I know, Mr Holmes, there was no word against him while he finished his studies.'

'And what about afterwards?' demanded Holmes. 'When he was assigned to a parish?'

The Italian smiled ruefully. 'There are nothing but good reports of him. For a good many years he was sent to poor parishes in the big cities, and always the reports of him are good. Wherever he went he was beloved of his parishioners and they wept to see him move on.'

'Perhaps he had turned over a new leaf,' I suggested. 'People do, you know.'

'Some people do, Doctor,' said Lestrade, 'but when a child is villainous it rarely changes. Show me a dishonest child and I'll show you a dishonest old man.'

Holmes smiled. 'You are, perhaps, a trifle cynical, Lestrade, but by and large I agree with your observation. Morality is absorbed early in life or not at all in my experience.'

I was shocked by the discussion and said so. 'What about,' I demanded, 'your Baker Street Irregulars, Holmes? Are you saying that they cannot be reformed? Surely you do not think so!'

My friend smiled again. 'No, no, Watson. I believe nothing but the best of my young assistants, but that is because they are not naturally corrupt or dishonest. I have selected them precisely because they are clever and ingenious and honest. Oh, I grant you that many a one of them has turned his hand to picking a pocket or stealing from a shop, but you will never find them stealing from their poor brothers. Salvatore Tosca seems to be of that different breed, who regard the whole world as constructed for their advantage. They, my friend, do not reform – they simply become more experienced and more cunning.'

The Italian detective had not understood our references to the Baker Street Irregulars, but he followed Holmes' comments on the Cardinal and nodded his head vigorously.

'Absolutely so, Mr Holmes. Absolutely so. I believe that he was merely awaiting his time. That time came when the Church sent him to the States. He was sent to a parish in Boston, and there he found his chance.'

'In what way?' asked Holmes.

'You must understand, Mr Holmes, that in big cities in the States the Catholic congregations have a lot of Italians and a lot of Irish, because these are good Catholic countries. In some cities there is more Irish and less Italians and in others there is more Italians and less Irish. In Boston there are lots of Irish, and it was them who provided his opportunity.'

He took a swallow of his brandy and looked around at us. 'You are all, I think, native Englishmen,' he continued, 'born in this country. Nobody will question your right to live and work here. It is not the same if you are an immigrant. There are many people who question your right to be in the country and want to drive you out or to limit what you can do. They treat immigrants like criminals, yet we would not be men if we did not do the best we can for ourselves and for our families, Mr Holmes. Should Irishmen and Italians and Jews stay at home and starve, when there is plenty to be had elsewhere?'

He shook his head and I noted the sad expression on his otherwise lively features and considered his own background as an immigrant child in America's metropolis.

'For this reason,' he went on, 'immigrants band together. In big cities there are areas of Irish, areas of Italians, areas of Jews, where they can feel at home among their own kind. It is out of such places that the Italian gangs of my city come – an attack by the lawless on those who try to suppress them. All that they do is to make the outcry against immigration worse.'

'And in Boston?' urged Holmes.

'In Boston it is mainly Irish immigration and they too have their gangs, but they have something else. In Boston the Irish have realized that no one will treat them properly so long as they have no power, so they have set about taking power in the city's politics.'

'And that,' interjected Holmes, 'is the power to which Tosca allied himself.'

Petrosino's face brightened. 'Exactly, Mr Holmes! That is just what he did. These Irish immigrants so anxious to make their way in politics were his congregation and he helped them make their way. He could persuade the rest of the Catholics in the city to vote for the Irish candidate, and he did so. In return, the Irish politicians saw that Tosca's church was never short of funds for any purpose he had in mind. It went on for years and it served both parties – the Irish became the biggest political force in Boston and Tosca became an outstanding figure in the Church in the States.'

'But he went to New York, did he not?' said Holmes.

Petrosino nodded. 'In the end his congregation – those who

were not Irish – realized that he had taken them out of the grip of the American-born and sold them to the Irish, and they began to mutter. No matter what his congregation thought, he had done what the Church deemed to be good work, so they responded to the complaints by promoting him and moving him to New York.'

'Promoting him?' I exclaimed.

'Oh yes, *Dottore*. He was promoted. Now maybe somebody also had a word with him about the Irish, because when he came to New York he went back to his own people and concerned himself with the Italians in the city. Still, he had tasted power in Boston and he went looking for it again. Now, the poor Italians in New York, they have no power nor money, but he soon found that there are Italians in New York with money and power – the gangsters.'

The little American had worked himself up to the point where he almost spat out his last word, then remembered where he was and glanced about him with an air of embarrassment.

'I apologize, gentlemen,' he said, 'but to think that these people are from the same country as me makes me very angry.'

'You were telling us about Tosca's adventures when he was promoted to New York,' Holmes urged.

'It was the same story as in Boston – only worse,' said the American detective. 'In Boston he dealt with people seeking political power and prepared to pay well for assistance – in New York he dealt with people seeking criminal profits, and they paid even better. He could raise more money than any other priest in the city, and I don't deny a lot of it went on good works, but a lot of it went into his own pocket and, as to where it came from – brothels and protection, forgery and boy houses, gambling and corruption! Still – there was a price to pay.'

Our interest quickened. 'What was that?' I asked.

He laughed hollowly. 'It was the friendship of Vito Corese. A very expensive burden.'

'And Corese is the man that you seek?' Holmes enquired.

Petrosino nodded. 'Vito Corese is the Ruler of the Rule of Nine. He is from an old Sicilian family who say that they were Mafia back in the French days. There are many such families in Italy, maybe forty or fifty in Sicily alone, and such people are left alone by the authorities. They bribe and blackmail magistrates and law officers, but Corese's crimes became so great that at last there were investigations of him and he went to the States and there he started again. First he started with protection – with extorting money from little shopkeepers in return for not attacking their shops. That has two purposes, it raises money quickly and it spreads terror of the organization, so that people will not speak out about it.'

He shook his head, sadly. 'Soon he had established his Rule of Nine, they had raised money and they were in business – vice, forgery, protection, blackmail, murder. You name it – they do it. Then along came Salvatore Tosca. He was the ideal mark for Corese, a man who was both corrupt and powerful. Oh, yes, Corese paid money to Tosca and in return Tosca supported him in every way. Priests provided alibis for criminals, properties we knew belonged to Corese's gang seemed to be owned by the Church, priests came to court and swore character references for the most damnable villains.'

'But you say that Corese exacted a price?' said Holmes.

'Oh, most certainly, Mr Holmes. Vito Corese does not believe in loyalty. He believes that he must grapple his associates to him with bonds of fear and self-interest. With Tosca, Corese soon smelt out his weakness for boys. The good priest used to visit Corese's boy houses in disguise, no doubt as a guest of the house, and once he started on that, he was Corese's creature entirely and would never refuse him, because Corese would have photographs or letters to a boy or simply boys who would recognize Tosca. There were things that Tosca did for Corese where he must have had his hand forced by such blackmail. Then, at last, the Church called Tosca to Rome to become a Cardinal Secretary and he was no longer my business, for which I was greatly relieved, but Vito Corese remains my business.'

'And your business, Detective, as you have explained,' said Holmes, 'is bringing Corese to book for murder in the United States. My business is avenging the callous slaying of Father Grant and the recovery of the Vatican Cameos if possible. Where is the thread that connects Corese and Tosca with the Cameos? While I have long suspected Cardinal Tosca of complicity in the theft, I have never understood his reasons. He is known to be personally wealthy and the Cameos are not a trophy that he might hang on the walls of his Vatican apartment.'

Petrosino smiled. 'The connecting thread, as you say, Mr Holmes, is Corese's passion. He loves to acquire rare and beautiful things. Once he made an attempt to steal one of the copies of the Declaration of Independence, but he was foiled. The Vatican Cameos are unique. As soon as he read of their discovery, he would long to possess them, and Cardinal Secretary Tosca would have been a malleable tool in Corese's hands for the reasons I have explained.'

Holmes nodded. 'I see,' he said, but if Corese stole the Cameos for his own possession, he will never let them go.'

'Ah, no,' said the American. 'Usually that would be so, but this is different. As soon as I knew of the crime, I realized that it was Corese, using his influence on Tosca. Since then I have been seeking a way to bring pressure upon them both and I think I have succeeded.'

'How have you done that?' asked my friend.

Nine

A Visit to the Clergy

Petrosino smiled widely. 'I had no means of applying pressure to Corese,' he said, 'but there was a way of frightening the good Cardinal.'

'What was that?' asked Lestrade.

'The same weapon that Corese used – the fear of exposure.'

'You blackmailed him?' said Holmes.

Petrosino smiled again, more widely. 'I suppose you might say that, Mr Holmes. It occurred to me that there were many in the Church in New York who understood what Salvatore Tosca is. Many of them deeply disapproved of his actions but had not sufficient power in the Church to stand up against him. I have sought out these people and made friends of them. I have spent much time telling them how I am certain that Corese blackmailed Tosca into helping him with his crime and that I am certain Corese has the Vatican Cameos. I have contrived to give them the impression that I am drawing closer to Corese and Tosca and that one day I shall make an arrest.'

'And the effect of all this?' asked Holmes.

'Has been to start a kind of panic. They have undoubtedly let it be known in Rome what I have told them. They will have expressed their fears to their colleagues at the Vatican and the word will have reached Cardinal Tosca. It is for that reason that the Cardinal has come to London – because he must try and recover the Cameos and put an end to any investigation.'

'Is that likely?' asked Lestrade. 'If, as you say, this Corese fellow makes a practice of collecting what he shouldn't have, surely he's not going to let the Cameos go?'

'It is never easy to do business with Don Vito Corese,' said the American, 'but Tosca will be desperate. At all costs he cannot afford an investigation which reveals his part in the plot. If, as I believe, the word I have planted has reached his colleagues in the College of Cardinals, they will be urging Tosca to do whatever is necessary to recover the Cameos and avoid an enormous scandal.'

'And what about the murder of Father Grant?' demanded Holmes. 'Do you believe that the Church proposes to forget that?'

'Oh,' said Petrosino, waving a hand. 'Tosca will hope to reach some arrangement with Corese whereby a couple of the Rule of Nine's *pisciotti* – the small fry of the gang – will be handed over to be tried. They may even be the ones who did it. More likely they will be luckless villains who have offended against one of the Rules.'

'But why would Corese do that?' persisted Lestrade.

'Because, *Ispettore*, he loves nothing so much as money and power. He was driven out of Sicily and I drove him out of New York. Here in London he is establishing a new empire, with considerable success. He does not want that jeopardized by anything. If he can force Tosca to make a sufficiently large offer for the Cameos and find a scapegoat or two, he will return them. The law will or will not hang his hapless henchmen, the Holy Father will have his priceless Cameos, Cardinal Tosca will be safe from exposure and Corese will have proved his power over Tosca yet again. After which he will continue his business of corrupting your capital.'

'Then,' declared Holmes, knocking out his pipe on the fender, 'we must see that their plans go awry. What are your plans?'

'I am still seeking Corese's whereabouts,' said the American. 'He is certainly here in England, most probably in London. I must know where he is so that we can frustrate any deal that he makes with the Cardinal. What will you do, Mr Holmes?'

'In the first place I shall add to the pressure you have brought to bear on Tosca. I shall pay a call on the Cardinal Archbishop and remind him of my suspicions of his colleague.'

'Be careful that you do not frighten Tosca away,' said Petrosino.

Holmes shook his head. 'I shall be careful, but if what you say is true, it is of the utmost importance that Tosca reaches an accommodation with Corese, so he will not leave London easily.'

'I have no fear that they will eventually reach an agreement, Mr Holmes. Tosca is an extremely wealthy man and a desperate one. 'Corese is not a fool and he will know to the last dollar how much he can extract from Tosca and what he must give in return.'

'But suppose Corese refuses to play and threatens to expose Tosca?' I argued, for I saw it as a real objection.

The American detective shook his head vigorously. 'Ah, no, no, no,' he said. 'That would be to throw away his hold over Tosca, and he would not do that unless he was desperate. No, no, this is just a business transaction between two crooks. Corese will agree in the end, though Tosca will find out afterwards that he has been bound more firmly to Corese's will.'

'Then,' said Holmes, looking around at the other two detectives, 'it behoves us to know when and where any dealings between the two take place.'

'Exactly,' said Petrosino. 'With this in mind I am finding out where Corese is hiding himself.'

'That could be hard,' observed Lestrade, 'in London.'

'Not for me,' said the American. 'I know that he operates through the organ-grinders, that they are his eyes and his ears. That is why I have become one. Soon I shall be asked to join in the game.'

'The gang's mark was on your lodgings,' observed Lestrade. 'Does your landlady know anything?'

Petrosino shook his head. 'Not she,' he said. 'I do not say she is the best landlady in the world, but she is not a part of the Rule of Nine. The mark is at her door to show that she has paid her protection. If you see that mark with one square or more filled in, that tells the collector that someone has not paid their dues.'

'Then,' said Holmes, rising from his chair, 'we must leave you to pursue Corese while we apply a little more pressure to His Eminence the Cardinal, but you must be careful, Detective. I agree with you that Benetti's organ warehouse is involved. The corpse in the tea chest was most probably placed in its coffin somewhere in close proximity to Lantern Lane, where the tea wholesalers are. I believe you may be very close to the heart of the conspiracy.'

'I hope so, very much,' replied Petrosino.

Holmes and I had intended to end our day with a visit to a concert and, shortly after our guests had left, we were making our way down Baker Street to the cab rank by Madame Tussaud's Exhibition.

I had paused to tighten the lace of a shoe and Holmes was a few steps ahead of me. At the kerbside stood a four-wheeler, its head towards the Marylebone Road and, as I straightened up, I saw Holmes come alongside the cab. As he did so, the door opened and I heard a voice ask him for directions. My friend stepped politely toward the cab's door and, in the next instant, he was struck over the head with some kind of cudgel and dragged into the vehicle.

I sprang up the street, calling for assistance, though there was nobody on the pavements. As I reached the growler its door was closing, but I seized its handle and tore it wide open. As I did so, two figures appeared behind me, apparently emerging from hiding behind the vehicle. I, too, was struck forcefully over the head and thrust into the cab. I have a dim recollection of tumbling on top of Holmes on the floor of the carriage before blackness descended on me.

How long it was before consciousness returned I do not

know, but I recovered to find myself propped upright along-side Holmes on a seat of the cab. Both my friend and I were bound hand and foot and gagged, while the two ruffians who had assaulted us sat opposite, watching us. The blinds of the carriage were drawn down and I could tell only that we were racing at a breakneck pace along cobbled streets. I had no idea in what part of the city we might be.

Holmes and I were helpless, but despite my throbbing head, I tried to observe our captors in the hope that, should I have the misfortune to meet them again, I should recognize them. They were, however, as nondescript a pair of roughs as you might find in the slums of any great city, one tall and bony with gingerish hair and the other stockier, more muscular and with a broad, weathered face topped by brown hair turning grey. So far as I could determine from the occasional mutterings exchanged between them, they were both British, though they had accents which might be Irish.

When I had assessed our captors, I tried to imagine what had given rise to the attack. If, as I thought, our guardians were Irish, I could see no reason for the in-cident. Holmes was not, to my knowledge, engaged in any matter with an Irish connection at the time. In my years at his side I had learned that it was only in the most important and complex of his enquiries that violence was directed against us, and I could recall no such matter at present.

I was occupying my aching head with these speculations when I became aware that our jehu was slowing down. Soon we felt the cab swerve to the right and the wheels begin to go over gravel rather than cobbles. We had evidently reached our destination.

The vehicle halted and one of our guards rose from his seat. Pulling a knife from the back of his belt, he slit the cords that bound our feet. Meanwhile his companion, the taller of the two, had produced an ugly snub-nosed revolver which he brandished at us.

'Get out, slowly!' he commanded, and now his Irish accent

was clear, 'but don't make any foolish movements. If you try to escape I'll drop your friend.'

Slowly, as the circulation returned to our cramped limbs, Holmes and I stepped down from the vehicle, our captors jumping down behind us. Looking about us, I saw that we were standing in front of a small Georgian house with a lawn stretching between us and the trees that bordered the road.

The gunman prodded me in the ribs with his weapon. 'March!' he commanded. 'And no stupidity!'

We were taken through the front door, across the hall and along a corridor towards the rear of the house, pausing at last outside a door.

The shorter ruffian knocked on the door and was answered by a curt 'Bring them in!' barked from inside.

We were led into a large, square room, apparently a library. Two tall windows pierced the wall opposite the door, but were closely curtained. To our right, a great banner hung between two bookcases, its colourful image depicting Saint George destroying the dragon. The room was lit by lamps, one on a table to our right and another on a broad desk that stood in the left-hand corner. A tall, pale-faced man sat at the desk. He stood up at our entry and it was possible to see that he was dressed in clerical black and wore the undivided collar of a clergyman.

The man pointed to two armchairs which stood opposite his desk. 'Put them in those!' he commanded his henchmen and, when Holmes and I had dropped gratefully into the seats, said, 'Good evening, Mr Holmes, Dr Watson.'

The tang of Northern Ireland was clear in the man's speech. I had been wondering who he might be, but his dress and accent, taken with the banner of Saint George, told me. Holmes was looking at our host with a faint twist of amusement to his mouth.

'Well, well,' he remarked, 'the so-called Reverend Hubert Cravat!'

The man glowered at Holmes. 'What do you mean,' he demanded, 'the "so-called Reverend"?'

'I mean,' said Holmes, 'that "Reverend" is a title of honour, and one to which I am not sure you are entitled. I do not know why you have reverence, or if it is something that should be honoured. Treating the term merely as a form of address for a member of the clergy, I am aware that your clerical degree is one unrecognized in Britain and obtained by post from an American college, while your Church of Saint George was founded by you, apparently as a device to enable you to take money from the gullible.'

'You would do well to curb your insolent tongue, Holmes,' snapped Cravat. 'If the Church of England is not prepared to protect our people from the tentacles of the Roman Whore, someone must do so, and it is for that reason that the Church of Saint George was founded. You are an educated man. You cannot be unaware that Britain was a Christian nation long before Gregory sent the poisonous Augustine here to enforce the rule of Rome.'

Holmes raised a hand. 'I do not deny the point,' he said, 'but if you were about to tell me that the present-day Protestant churches are descended from the old Celtic Church, they are not. They are descended from the English Catholic Church created by Henry VIII and turned into a Protestant church by his daughter, Elizabeth – apart from those of more recent and even more dubious lineage, like your own. Please spare us any historical lecture and any sermon which you had prepared and let us know why we have been so peremptorily summoned. It was not necessary, you know. A postcard to Baker Street would have brought us along.'

'I needed to be certain I had your full attention,' said Cravat.

'If you have something to say, Cravat, get on with it!' urged Holmes.

The purported clergyman waved a thick finger at my friend. 'You,' he said, 'have involved yourself in the affair of the Vatican Cameos.'

'Wrong,' replied Holmes. 'At the time of the murder of Father Grant and the disappearance of the Cameos, I was consulted by the Morence family and their insurers. The Cameos have not been found, *ergo* my commission still exists.'

'And you believe you can recover them – after so long?' demanded Cravat.

'I make no excuse to you, Cravat, when I say that I failed to recover them earlier because of the obstruction of a certain organization.'

'Aha!' exclaimed Cravat. 'The Roman Church!'

Holmes remained silent.

'And you think you will succeed now where you failed before?'

'Let us say that I see a possible way through the entanglements now,' said Holmes. 'But what is your interest in the Cameos? Oh, I know you told the world that they would never be handed over to Cardinal Tosca and, but for your carelessness with a bucket of orange paint, you would have been the prime suspect, but they did not reach the Vatican and whoever has them seems to have done your work for you.'

'But he has not,' said Cravat, 'for I intended more than to prevent them reaching the Vatican. Those damned slips of ivory are revered by the foolish, the ungodly and the perverse, Mr Holmes, and I shall put an end to them. Those images of traitors, worshipped by followers of the Roman Whore, shall be destroyed, and their ashes I shall be pleased to send to Rome.'

'And you sent for me,' remarked Holmes, 'in your somewhat peremptory fashion, in order to warn me that the Cameos must be handed to you?'

'I did no such thing!' exclaimed the Irishman, failing to see Holmes' joke. 'I sent for you to impress it upon you that I will have them, and you will stand in my way at your peril!'

'I see,' acknowledged Holmes. 'And do you know where they are?'

'At this moment, I do not.'

'And do you know who stole them?'

'I do not, though I know you suspect Cardinal Tosca.'

'I suspect Cardinal Tosca of playing a part in the theft,' said Holmes. 'I know that he did not steal them. Do you know why Tosca is back in London?'

'I do not, but I am having him closely watched.'

'You would achieve more by listening to organ-grinders,' said Holmes. 'I have to say that it seems extremely unlikely that you will ever lay your hands on the Cameos.'

Cravat bent low over his desk and his eyes glittered in the lamplight. 'Make no mistake about it, Mr Holmes. I will have the Vatican Cameos and His Holiness will have their ashes. Now you may go!'

He issued instructions to his two louts and soon we were freed from our bonds and driven back to Baker Street as though we had been two honoured guests.

Ten

A Foreign Visitor

After the ministrations of Cravat's louts I was more than ready to lay my aching head upon a pillow, but on our return to Baker Street we were soon attended by Mrs Hudson, to tell us that a foreign gentleman had called shortly after our departure. On being told we were out for the evening he had at first elected to wait, then decided to return later.

'Was he a tall gentleman?' Holmes asked, and our landlady confirmed that he was.

'I'm afraid that he left no card,' she said, 'nor would he state his business.'

'Never mind, Mrs Hudson,' said my friend. 'Now, I think that both Dr Watson and I would be the better for a pot of tea, if we might trouble you before you retire?'

The tea did a little to relieve my head and make me a touch more alert.

'What tall foreigner are you expecting, Holmes?' I asked after a while.

'The owner of that stick beside your chair,' he replied. 'Really, Watson, I sometimes think we might make a comfortable living from disposing of the hats and sticks that our callers leave behind. Still, they provide me with material on which I can test my deductive methods.'

'Why do you say that he was tall?' I asked, looking at the silver-mounted stick beside my chair.

'Because, Watson, even from here I can see that the stick is a good two inches longer than that of the average Englishman

– almost as long as my own. It follows, therefore, that our visitor is likely to be as tall as me.'

He stepped across the room and took up the stick, examining it closely, even unscrewing its head a little way. Then he drew his lens from his pocket and examined the head and foot of the stick before leaning it against the fireplace.

'And what does it tell you?' I enquired.

'That we may shortly be visited by a tall man with waxed moustaches, a military bearing and hair cut in the short, Prussian fashion.'

'A German!' I exclaimed.

Holmes shook his head, impatiently. 'No, no, Watson. You have evidently not followed my train of thought. Our visitor is almost certainly a Swiss gentleman.'

'You cannot,' I complained, 'deduce all that from the stick,' though I knew as I spoke the words that he would soon prove to me that he could.

'We have Mrs Hudson's confirmation of the stick's implication that the man is tall. Mrs Hudson called him a foreigner and the craftsman who made that silver head was not British. Indeed, if you apply my lens you will see on the band the name "Bern" as the place of manufacture.'

'So he is Swiss,' I conceded, 'but the waxed moustaches, short haircut and military bearing – what leads you to those suppositions?'

'They are far more than suppositions,' he said, sternly. 'The head of the stick unscrews, because it is a swordstick. Caught in the thread of the head are a few very short fragments of hair, so cut at the requirement of a man who has his short hair cut frequently. Such a man will wear the waxed moustaches that usually accompany the haircut.'

'But the military bearing,' I said. 'If he requires a stick he will have some degree of infirmity.'

'Well done, Watson. An important point, but a false one. Examination of the tip of his stick reveals that the wear is even at the front and the rear, not on either side. A man who uses his stick for support will create uneven wear, on one side or the other. This gentleman carries a stick as a potential weapon or as an adjunct of his dress and swings it regularly as he takes long strides.'

I snorted, still not entirely convinced. Holmes smiled and stepped to the window, drawing the curtain aside a little.

'If you doubt my conclusions,' he said, 'you will soon be able to test them. A carriage is drawing up outside and a tall gentleman getting out.'

The night bell rang vigorously and I heard the page run down to the door. Only moments later he showed into the room a man who met exactly Holmes' prognostications. Our visitor had steely grey eyes and was wrapped in a light cape.

'Ah!' exclaimed Holmes. 'Mr Jakov Lindt!'

Our visitor drew back slightly. 'Have we met before, Mr Holmes?' he enquired, with only the slightest of foreign intonations.

'No, sir, but I am aware that you are the Capo dell'Ufficio Centrale Vigilanza at the Vatican, and this morning's paper told me that you had called on the Cardinal Archbishop of Westminster yesterday. Pray take the basket chair, you may find it the most comfortable.'

Lindt lowered his considerable length into the basket chair, but still watched Holmes with a wary expression. 'That does not explain,' he said, 'how you come to recognize me at sight.'

Holmes laughed. 'You were unlucky enough to leave your handsome swordstick behind and I have been exercising my mind in constructing an image of the stick's owner.' He took up the stick and rehearsed his deductions, while Lindt watched him expressionlessly.

'You are a very clever man,' he said, when my friend had finished and given him his stick.

'And what brought the chief of the Central Vigilance Office at the Vatican to see me so late at night, Mr Lindt? It was surely not so that I could entertain you with mental parlour tricks?'

I had been racking my brains to understand the Swiss connection, and now realized that our visitor was the head of the Pope's Swiss Guard – in effect the Vatican's Chief of Police and Commander of its Army.

'His Eminence, the Cardinal Archbishop, sent for me as a matter of the greatest urgency,' Lindt began, 'because he wished me to talk to you about the Vatican Cameos.'

'I wonder,' said Holmes, 'why His Eminence, who has had face-to-face dealings with me in the past, should find it necessary, on this occasion, to summon you from Rome, Mr Lindt?'

'Because, Mr Holmes, he says that you and he have discussed this matter before, and that you failed to understand his viewpoint. It was his feeling that if I, carrying the responsibilities that I do, were to call upon you, you might be more ready to accept His Eminence's view in this affair.'

'If,' said Holmes, 'the arguments of the Church's highest functionary in Britain – a man well known to me – have failed to move me, it implies no disrespect when I suggest that your journey has been wasted. You speak of the Cardinal Archbishop's viewpoint. What we are discussing is the brutal murder of a young priest and the theft of a priceless treasure. What legitimate viewpoint can there possibly be, other than that the murderers should be brought to justice and their booty recovered?'

'Ah, if it were only that simple, Mr Holmes!' said our guest.

'It is precisely and entirely that simple,' said Holmes and took up his pipe from the table.

'If the Cameos were the property of a private or commercial organization, Mr Holmes, I would agree with you absolutely, but here the interests of the Church are at stake.'

Holmes was filling his meerschaum. 'Why,' he demanded, 'are the interests of the Church different from those of any civilized person? Does His Holiness not desire that justice should be done?'

'I have not,' said Lindt, 'had the pleasure of discussing this matter with His Holiness, but I have listened to the Cardinal Archbishop on the subject at great length.'

'And his view is?' demanded Holmes.

'It is His Eminence's view that it would be unwise, in attempting to deal with the theft and murder, to give ammunition to the Church's enemies.'

'And why does he think I might do that?'

'Because he fears that you still believe that a senior member of the Church was somehow involved in the matter.'

'You mean Cardinal Tosca?' asked Holmes.

Our visitor seemed almost to wince at Holmes' blunt introduction of the name.

'Yes,' he agreed, reluctantly. 'Cardinal Tosca, if you will.'

'His Eminence has no doubt made it clear to you that I do not suspect Cardinal Tosca of taking part in theft and murder, only of facilitating them, and I am prepared to accept that he was almost certainly unaware that the robbers intended to kill Father Grant,' said my friend. 'My concern is not with the Cardinal. The Church can deal with him or not, as it chooses. My intention is to bring to book the killers of Father Grant and, if possible, recover the Cameos. I cannot see why that should worry you or the Cardinal Archbishop.'

Our visitor nodded slowly. 'Put like that it all seems very reasonable,' he agreed, 'but let us suppose you succeed and the killers stand trial in England. There will be nothing to prevent them saying that Cardinal Tosca was a part of the plot – not to say its progenitor. Even if they could not prove it, that would be a story which would fly round the world in an instant, and wherever it went it would be used as a stick to beat the Church by her enemies. Cardinal Tosca is the most senior of His Holiness's *uomini di fiducia* – his men of trust, his advisors.'

'The Church will have her enemies, Mr Lindt, whatever you or I do,' said Holmes, 'as she has had her enemies in the past. Nevertheless, the Church exists and grows. As to the Cardinal, one day His Holiness will lose the benefit of Cardinal Tosca's advice, in any case. The Church will no doubt survive without it.'

The Swiss nodded. 'There is no difficulty that the Church would not survive,' admitted Lindt, 'but this is, nevertheless, one that would not easily be forgotten and which we would seek to avoid if at all possible.'

'And just how do you propose it can be avoided?' demanded Holmes, cramming tobacco into his pipe with unusual vigour.

Our guest folded his hands over the top of his handsome stick and looked earnestly at Holmes. 'If,' he said, 'you were to succeed in establishing the identity of the killers, and if you were able to reclaim the Cameos, I would be happy to accept your word that the murderers had been dealt with properly, Mr Holmes.'

I had been aware for some time that, beneath his calm exterior, Sherlock Holmes was growing very angry. I fully expected his anger to flare up after Lindt's extraordinary proposal, but it did not.

'How very kind of you,' said Holmes, icily. 'Has this offer the blessing of the Cardinal Archbishop?'

Our guest shook his head. 'Our discussion ended with him giving me carte blanche to reach whatever accommodations were necessary to see justice done for Father Grant and, if possible, recover the Cameos, without involving the Church in any scandal. The proposal is my own.'

'A proposal,' said Holmes, 'that I should commit murder to avoid embarrassment to the Church? Is that not what you have just put to me?'

Lindt was silent and Holmes uncoiled himself from his chair. 'I believe that our discussion is at an end,' he said. 'I do not know in what terms you may be required to report back to the Cardinal Archbishop, but you may certainly tell him that you have failed to reach agreement with me. Whether you repeat your shameful proposal to him is a matter for you. Goodnight, Mr Lindt,' and he swung open the door.

Lindt left without a further word. Holmes flung himself back into his chair and applied a match to his pipe, taking a long draw at it with firmly clenched jaws.

'Blessed are ye when men shall persecute you,' I quoted jokingly, when I saw that his anger had subsided a little.

'Amen to that, Watson,' he said. 'Amen to that.'

Eleven

Parsley and Chestnuts

If my head had recovered a little by morning, it was not helped by the rattle of traffic in the street and the whistling of errand boys, augmented by a barrel organ close to our premises, remorselessly grinding out one of Sullivan's popular airs.

I was late down to breakfast and somewhat less than my best, though I found Sherlock Holmes seated at the table in a dressing gown, with the usual litter of morning papers about him.

'Good morning, Watson!' he greeted me, cheerfully enough despite our misadventures of the previous day. 'I fear that Cravat's hooligans did you more damage than you acknowledged last night.'

I rubbed the back of my head, where a large swelling had risen. 'It will pass,' I said, 'though I could do with a quieter street at the moment.'

Holmes removed several sheets of the papers from the table as I seated myself. 'Hearing your foot on the stair,' he said, 'I took the liberty of asking Mrs Hudson to provide some more toast and replenish the tea.'

He had hardly spoken when our landlady made her appearance with a tray, enquiring what I would like for breakfast.

'I think tea and toast will be quite sufficient this morning, Mrs Hudson,' I said, and noted that Holmes was scribbling on a page of his pocketbook.

'Please have the boy take this to the organ-grinder outside,' requested Holmes, giving Mrs Hudson the note together with a small coin. 'It seems that Dr Watson is not in musical mood this morning.'

Mrs Hudson left and I busied myself with tea and toast. Holmes continued leafing through the papers, and soon began whistling to himself.

I stood it for a little while, but felt driven to complain at last. 'Holmes,' I objected, 'what was the point of trying to silence the organ-grinder, only to start whistling the same tune. I should be enormously grateful if you could read your newspapers in silence.'

He folded his newspaper shut and smiled at me affably. 'My dear Watson!' he exclaimed, 'I am so sorry! I was merely trying, in a rather unsubtle fashion, to draw your attention to the peculiar aptness of the organ-grinder's choice. How do the words run?' and he began to sing: 'When the enterprising burglar's not a-burgling, not a-burgling, And the cut-throat isn't occupied in crime.'

'Alright, Holmes!' I protested. 'I am fully familiar with *The Pirates of Penzance.*'

No sooner had I spoken than the music outside ended and, minutes later, Mrs Hudson appeared again, introducing Detective Petrosino in his character as Sandro Parselli.

'Ah!' cried Holmes. 'Welcome, Detective Petrosino! Pray take the basket chair. Mrs Hudson, I believe our visitor will prefer coffee to tea.'

Once the American had been supplied with coffee and a cheroot, Holmes put away his bundle of newspapers. 'I hope,' he said, 'that your appearance here indicates that there has been a development or some success in your enquiries.'

The stocky detective puffed contentedly at his cheroot and smiled. 'Oh yes, Mr Holmes. I think I can say that I have had some success in my enquiries. Now I know where Corese lives.'

Holmes eyes widened and he rubbed one hand against the other, always an indication that his interest was aroused.

'Really?' he said. 'And how have you come by that information?'

'You will understand, Mr Holmes, that since I came to London I have been at great pains to make myself out as a person who can be trusted. Once I had discovered that Corese's protection rackets were run through the organ-grinders, I took up that profession. I hired my instrument from Benetti's warehouse, like all of the Italian organ-grinders in London, and I kept my eyes and ears open.'

He sipped his coffee. 'So,' he said, 'I knew that the Rule of Nine passed its orders through Benetti's warehouse, and very soon I was able to work out who the gang trusted and who it didn't. By no means all of the people who work for Benetti or hire his organs are part of the Rule of Nine. For example, a lot of the organ-grinders do Corese's dirty work, but so far as I can see none of the hokey-pokey sellers are a part of it, though they hire their carts from Benetti like the organ men. I have got to the point where people are used to me at the warehouse. They will not trust me with their secrets yet, but they talk to me and they gossip in front of me. By this means I learn little pieces of things that I can put together.'

Holmes nodded, but I saw that he was growing impatient.

'Now the other organ-grinders and the warehouse men, they tell me that the business is owned by the man they call "Old Benetti". He is, indeed, an old man. They say that not so long ago they thought he was going out of business. He was not buying new organs, the old ones were only cheaply repaired and patched up and he kept putting up the price of hiring. Old Benetti looked worried all the time, and everyone thought he was going bust.'

He took a swallow of coffee and smiled at Holmes and me.

'But then,' he said, 'things started to look up – new organs, proper repairs, lower prices for hiring, everything looking good.'

'And why was that?' I asked.

'That, *Dottore*, was because of Old Benetti's nephew.'

'His nephew?' interjected Holmes.

Petrosino nodded. '*Si*, his nephew – or so he says. The

people say that Old Benetti said that his nephew had come from Sicily and had put new money into the business and now everything was going to go well.'

'And you believe,' said my friend, 'that this so-called nephew of Old Benetti is your man – Vito Corese.'

'That is exactly what I suspect,' confirmed the American. 'The people also say that although everything now goes well, the old man still looks worried all the time. As to his nephew, they never see him at the warehouse, but there are always messages to Old Benetti from him. I believe that, whether he is Benctti's nephew or not, Vito Corese is hiding behind Benetti's business and blackmailing Old Benetti into letting him use the business as a front for his protection racket.'

'That sounds very likely,' said Holmes, enthusiastically. 'Tell me, have you, yourself, seen Benetti's nephew?'

The American detective shook his head. 'No,' he said. 'Which is good, because Corese knows me from New York. But I have a clue that the nephew is Corese.'

'What is that?' asked Holmes.

'Someone who has seen him told me that young Benetti has a finger missing, but he could not recall which one.'

'And Corese has a finger missing?' Holmes asked.

'I am sorry, Mr Holmes. I should have told you before. Don Vito Corese has the pinkie of his left hand – the little finger, I think you call it – missing. It is the reason for the name of his gang. His finger was chopped off when he was a boy in the gangs, to discipline him, so his friends started to call him "Nine Fingers", then just "Nine". When he set up his own gang, he called it the "Rule of Nine" so that everyone who remembered him would know who was in charge of it.'

'It would be unwise,' said Holmes, 'for you to get close enough to the nephew to identify him as Corese, but that is something that I can do.'

'How will you do that, Mr Holmes?' asked Petrosino.

Holmes ignored the question. 'Tell me,' he said, 'how do the nephew's messages reach the warehouse at Lantern Street?'

'Sometimes they come by telegraph in a kind of code, sometimes they are brought by messenger boys.'

'Have you any idea where they come from?' persisted Holmes.

'Not really,' said Petrosino. 'I have heard people say that he lives outside London, in the country, perhaps in Surrey, but nobody seems to be sure. They say that some people go and see him at his home, but these are people I dare not talk to.'

'Of course not,' agreed Holmes, 'but do not worry, Detective. Your colleagues at Scotland Yard have their uses and one of them is overriding official barriers. I am sure we can persuade Lestrade to get those telegrams quietly intercepted and their source noted. Once we know his whereabouts, I can pay him a visit and confirm your impression.'

'That would be very dangerous, Mr Holmes!' exclaimed the little American. 'He must know who you are and what you do.'

Holmes chuckled. 'Do not worry, Detective. I shall not call on him as Sherlock Holmes, Consulting Detective. You are not the only practitioner of disguise in this room.'

Petrosino nodded, seemingly satisfied.

'Besides,' Holmes continued, 'it is not just a question of looking for a missing left little finger; I wish to see where he lives and how he lives, by way of considering where the Vatican Cameos may be.'

Petrosino had finished his coffee and rose. 'Then I shall leave that part to you,' he said, 'and carry on as usual.'

'If I were you,' said Holmes, 'I would be a little more cautious than usual. You know that you are always in great danger. If I can discover where Corese lives, without any further danger to you, I suggest that you simply continue your organ-grinding business but be careful of talking about Benetti's affairs or his nephew's.'

'That is good advice, Mr Holmes,' said our visitor, and taking his battered straw hat he left us.

As soon as he had gone Holmes rubbed his hands together

and smiled. 'This is excellent, Watson!' he declared. 'What a singularly useful fellow is that little Italian. He is worth half the fools at Scotland Yard. Now, Watson, we must make a plan.'

'A plan for what?' I asked.

'Why, a plan that will take us into the home of Don Vito Corese, Watson. First I must wire Lestrade to have his telegrams intercepted. We can achieve nothing until we have Corese's address.'

He took out his pocketbook, scribbled a few lines and tucked the paper into his breast pocket.

'I can send that on my way,' he said.

'On your way where?' I asked. 'Would you like me to accompany you?'

'No, no, Watson. There is no need on this occasion. Besides, you really do look a little the worse for wear after yesterday's adventures. It will do you good to spend a quiet day with a good book.'

He was more than half right, but I still resented being left behind.

'But where will you be?' I said.

'I,' said Sherlock Holmes, 'am going to see a man about chestnuts.'

'Chestnuts!' I exclaimed, completely bewildered.

'Chestnuts, Watson,' he repeated and left.

Twelve

A Cycling Expedition

I had little alternative but to follow Holmes' advice and spend my day with a book. The volume I chose was such a poor selection that, when Mrs Hudson came to lay tea, she found me asleep in my armchair.

'You must have needed it, Doctor,' she said, when I apologized. 'To tell you the truth, I thought you were not looking your best at breakfast, when you only took toast.'

As a medical man I was growing somewhat tired of receiving laymen's diagnoses, and I was glad when she changed the topic.

'Do you know, Doctor, if Mr Holmes will be in for tea?'

I laughed. 'You know him as well as I do, Mrs Hudson. All I can tell you is that he left this morning to see a man about chestnuts. If it is no great trouble to you, I suggest you lay for both of us. He may turn up at any moment.'

Mrs Hudson looked at me with a puzzled frown. 'But chestnuts aren't even in season, Doctor,' she said.

Despite her perplexity, she followed my suggestion and hardly was the table laid when I heard familiar footsteps bounding up the stairs. Holmes appeared at the door, clutching a large roll of paper under one arm.

'Capital!' he said. 'Capital! I have been so busy today I have barely supped and not dined.'

Dropping the bundle of papers on his writing desk he dropped into a chair at the table. Mrs Hudson returned with the tea tray at that exact moment, and Holmes was quick to assist her in unloading the tray and pouring tea for both of us. He drank his cup down in long draughts and immediately poured himself a second.

'That's better!' he said, after he had drunk half the second cup. 'Do you know, Watson, I have had nothing since breakfast except two large glasses of Scandinavian gin.'

I ignored the temptation to question the Scandinavian connection. It has always been my observation that, when bent on the solution of a problem, Holmes' appetite for anything except tobacco would disappear. Conversely, once a solution had been found, he could match the best of trenchermen. I perceived that he was in high good humour and waited until he was ready to tell me his news, which turned out to be after three soft-boiled eggs and numerous muffins with ginger conserve.

At last he wiped his lips, dropped his napkin and leaned back from the table, groping in his pocket for his briar.

'Well, Watson,' he began. 'I have been remiss. What sort of a day have you had?'

'Uneventful,' I said. 'Whereas you have evidently met with success.'

'I have indeed,' he confirmed. 'On my way home I took the opportunity to call at the Yard. Lestrade has come up trumps. I have the address of Young Benetti.'

He peered at his shirt cuff, where he had evidently written it, and read it out, 'The Villa Fiorelli, Spring Lane, Baxted, Surrey.'

'That's very good,' I agreed.

'Better yet, Watson. You and I have an appointment with Signor Benetti, as he styles himself.'

'An appointment!' I echoed, gaping like a fool. 'Why on earth would Corese wish to see us?'

'Oh, come, come,' said Holmes. 'I have not made it in the name of Sherlock Holmes and Dr Watson. Do credit me with a little sense, Watson. My wire was signed "Sigerson" and suggested that I was in a position to make him a lot of money. That is, I believe, what interests him and, accordingly, he has accepted. We shall see him tomorrow.'

'But what about?' I pursued him. 'On what pretext?'

'Ah,' he smiled, drawing deeply on his pipe. 'That is where the chestnuts come in.'

The stage lost a magnificent performer when Holmes took up detection. Apart from his uncanny ear for voices and accents and his magical ability to disguise himself, he had a conjurer's love of concealing the mechanisms by which his effects were created, leaving his audience to wonder. Before I could press any enquiry about chestnuts he adroitly turned the conversation to the recent increase in cab fares, so I remained perplexed and unsatisfied.

My perplexity deepened later in the evening. I had bidden him goodnight and was about to turn in, when he said, 'Ah, that reminds me. I had almost forgotten to ask. You can ride a bicycle, can you not?'

'A bicycle?' I said. 'I have not sat astride one since my teens.'

'I thought you would be able,' he said. 'I understand that the technique, once acquired, enters so deeply into the interior of the mind that it is never forgotten. In any case, you will have a little opportunity to practise.'

'Why,' I asked, 'is it necessary for me to ride a bicycle?' I was telling the truth when I had told him that my last close acquaintance with such a machine had been with one of the primitive devices of my youth and I did not recall the occasion with any great pride.

'Because,' he replied, 'I took the opportunity of purchasing two reliable second-hand machines today and had them forwarded by rail to Guildford, to await us in the morning. Goodnight, Watson.'

I was before him at breakfast in the morning. Having forgotten his remarks about concealing his identity, I was the more surprised when he made his appearance. He was stooped and wore thick pebble spectacles, while his hair was considerably greyed and dishevelled. His face was pale and dark hollows hung beneath his eyes. Normally a neat, perhaps prim, dresser, he was clad in an ill-fitting suit, seemingly of foreign cut, from the breast pocket of which protruded a cluster of pencils and what seemed to be one end of an engineer's folding boxwood rule. He greeted me in the soft accents of Scandinavia.

'Good morning, Holmes,' I responded. 'Pray tell me in what persona you are appearing today, and in what character I shall have to support you.'

He looked at me over his spectacles. 'I have become Arne Sigerson, Watson, a Norwegian engineer. You will be my commercial agent in England, Mr Wilson. It does not require much of you, though I think a billycock hat might aid the deception, if you do not object. A billycock seems to smack much more of the commercial than the professional man.'

'And what about these infernal bicycles?' I asked.

'Ah, yes,' he said. 'Mr Sigerson is a poor inventor, and Mr Wilson is not very successful. Neither can afford their own carriage, or even a cab from Guildford. Hence, I am afraid, we shall make the journey from Guildford to Baxted by velocipede.'

So it was that, a couple of hours later, I found myself perched uncomfortably on the saddle of a bicycle, pursuing Holmes through the lanes of Surrey. He was pedalling effortlessly, despite the bundle of papers that he clutched under one arm.

It was with no little relief that I saw Holmes turn aside from the road and lead us to a wayside inn. As I complained that the unfamiliar exercise had awakened pains in my injured leg and shoulder, my friend was all solicitude, urging me into a window seat in the bar and going to fetch us a drink.

I saw him in earnest conversation with a group of local labourers as the landlord pulled our drinks. When Holmes returned with the ale I sank a large draught with gratitude.

'There is no social facility anywhere in the world,' I remarked when I had removed the Surrey dust from my throat, 'that stands comparison with the wayside inns of England.'

Holmes smiled. 'Oh, indeed,' he agreed. 'As sources of local information they are excellent. Our fellow customers have confirmed that the villa is a little under a mile ahead. Do drink up, Watson. We have an appointment.'

The countryside through which we rode was typical of rural England, though rather less populated than one might have expected, but Corese's villa, when we reached it, was a surprise.

It stood under a fold of the Downs, surrounded by tall, dark trees, which screened it entirely from the road. An ornate double gate of wrought iron stood well back under the trees and seemed to be the only entrance.

Holmes turned his cycle through the gate and I followed, finding myself on a long drive, almost entirely overshadowed by the same dark trees that concealed the house. We had travelled some two hundred yards along the drive before we emerged from the trees and could see Corese's country home.

It was a wide, rectangular building, facing on to lawns dotted with gaudy flower beds and what appeared to be copies of classical statuary. The house itself was of cream stone, and so styled as to appear very exotic in the heart of rural Surrey, its facade heavily festooned with balconies, ornamental ironwork and even statuary. Holmes brought his machine to a halt in front of a set of wide steps and I followed suit. We removed our bicycle clips and approached the front door.

Within minutes a pretty maid had shown us into a sumptuous room which seemed to be a combination of library and study. The walls were lined with row upon row of expensively bound volumes and a quick glance showed me that they were almost all classic texts. At the same time, the rich leather and gilt bindings glowed as if new and showed no signs of regular use. The spaces between the bookshelves were filled with drawings and paintings, in decorative gilded frames. I do not pretend to be a connoisseur of art, but even my inexperienced eye recognized that all were original and some of the finest practitioners were represented. Pedestals here and there bore busts and small statues and a large and ornate desk stood with its back to the wide window.

Holmes was moving from one picture to another with small sounds of delight, and had just drawn my attention to what appeared to be a da Vinci drawing, when the door opened.

'Good morning, gentlemen!' said a voice which even my ear recognized as overlaid with Italian and American intonations. 'I see you approve of my little collection of pictures.'

We turned to meet the speaker. He was younger than I had expected, only in his thirties, and was informally clad in a red satin smoking jacket, tied with a sash, a smoking cap, plain trousers and Turkish slippers. Although he smiled at us, his lean dark features seemed to me so saurian as to chill at a glance.

Holmes stepped forward and shook our host's extended hand.

'Signor Benetti,' he said. 'I am Arne Sigerson and this is Mr Wilson, my commercial agent in England. As to your collection, even an engineer must have some appreciation of beautiful things, and you have so many in this one room.'

The Italian smiled. 'It is good of you to say so,' he said. 'I am not ashamed to say that I began life very poor, but I have made my way in the world and I have tried to surround myself with things that inspire. Let me show you some of my little beauties.'

He took Holmes by the elbow and walked us around the large room while he pointed out various rare first editions, paintings and pieces of sculpture. When he had done, we repeated the circuit, while he pulled open drawers of the cabinets that stood below his bookcases. Now we saw collections of ancient coins, rare butterflies, curious and old-fashioned seals, small ritual items of Roman and Egyptian pattern, and many more obscure, rare and extremely valuable items. The room was at once an office and a treasure house.

At last he seated himself at his huge desk and waved us to two chairs, offering us cigars as he did so.

'Now, gentlemen,' he said, once we had all lighted up, 'you have seen that I spend my money as fast as I make it. So, Mr Sigerson, when someone tells me that he can make me more, I have to hear what he has to say. What is your proposal?'

Holmes had kept his bundle of papers with him throughout, and now he began to unroll one on to the desktop, securing its corners with an unusual jade ashtray, a solid gold paperknife which seemed to have begun life with some darker purpose, and a small figure of some Roman deity.

'Mr Benetti,' he said, as he spread out the document. 'I understand that your firm is the biggest supplier of barrel organs and ice-cream carts for hire in Britain. Is that so?'

Benetti nodded. 'You are correct,' he confirmed.

'But you are not,' continued Holmes, as he took his seat, 'the only such supplier in the metropolis, I believe?'

'Once again, you are correct. There are a half dozen smaller firms.'

'And your business is seasonal – that is to say the demand for ice cream and for street music is a summer one?'

'Of course,' agreed Benetti.

'What would you say to a device that no competitor will have and that gives you a solid trade in the winter, Signor Benetti?'

Holmes had been leaning forward over his paper. Now he sat back and flung out a hand across the document.

'Let me show you, if I may,' he said, 'the plans of Sigerson's Pommarronier, a device which will heat chestnuts to the required temperature without the dirt, inconvenience and danger of a brazier, which will also roast potatoes and heat sausages, and which eliminates the wear upon materials caused by the heat of a brazier and the tedious business of starting up the brazier each time the device is taken on to the streets.'

I cannot speak for Benetti, but I was profoundly impressed. He seemed so, for he leaned forward to examine the drawing Holmes had spread, placing his left hand on its edge. It was clear that his little finger was missing.

Thirteen

A Twist of Fate

L ess than an hour and a half later Holmes and I were back at the inn along the road from Corese's Villa, taking a belated luncheon of bread and ham.

'So, Holmes,' I said, 'we have confirmed that Benetti is almost certainly Corese and that Petrosino's description of him as a mad collector is true. Where does that take us?'

'We have done more than that,' he said. 'We have established that he is Corese, and I now have a pretty fair idea of the whereabouts of the Vatican Cameos.'

'Why are you so certain that he is Corese, apart from the missing finger, I mean?'

'Watson!' chided Holmes. 'Consider the facts. The Rule of Nine appears to operate out of Old Benetti's warehouse. Old Benetti has taken on a partner, allegedly a nephew, who is never seen at the warehouse. We have confirmed that Old Benetti's so-called nephew is a man who is missing the little finger of the left hand, and a man who is an obsessive collector of rarities. What is more, Young Benetti steals.'

'How can you say so?' I asked.

'Because, Watson, unless I am very wide of the mark, the da Vinci drawing hanging on his wall is the very one stolen from the Duke of Pelsall's collection some four years ago.'

'And you mean he has the effrontery to display it on his wall?' I exclaimed.

'Oh, I imagine that he is pretty careful to ensure that he is not visited at home by anyone whom he fears or suspects.'

'Then, if he is so cool as to show the da Vinci, why does he not display the Vatican Cameos?'

Holmes favoured me with an impatient frown. 'Because, Watson, the Vatican Cameos are notorious and because murder was done in the acquisition of them. If he is ever challenged over the da Vinci, or any other piece in his collection, he will have some story about acquiring it from a stranger – some tale that can be neither proved nor disproved. He could never say that of the Cameos, so they remain concealed.'

'And where do you think they are?'

'In his safe, I would suggest,' replied Holmes.

'I saw no safe,' I said.

This time his frown was even more impatient. 'Would you expect it to be standing in the middle of the room, Watson? It is behind the small Fragonard, to the right of his desk.'

'How do you know?' I asked.

'Because,' he said, impatiently, 'Benetti is a cigar smoker and on both sides of the frame of the Fragonard there are traces of cigar ash on the gilt, no doubt from his taking the frame in both hands to swivel it aside and gain access to his safe. He should instruct his maids to run a duster over that frame every night.'

'Are you sure of your conclusions?' I asked. 'It is a large house. He might have a strongroom or vault elsewhere in the building.'

'He might,' said Holmes, shortly, 'but he does not.'

My surprised face spoke my question for me and he relented.

'When we called here this morning, Watson, I asked directions from the locals. I also took the opportunity to discuss my business with Mr Benetti, discovering thereby that two of my acquaintances had worked on the building of the Villa. I expressed concern as to the safety of my invaluable chestnut-cooker plans and a hope that Benetti had a strongroom. They regretted telling me that he has only a wine cellar beneath the house and no strongroom above ground.'

I chuckled, and a thought occurred to me. 'Tell me,' I said, 'does Sigerson's Pommarronier really do all that you claimed for it?'

'So far as I know,' he said. 'The drawings belong to poor Arthur Swinby, who spends his days in a wretched garret in Whitechapel, hunched over a drawing board while he devises machines like the electric chestnut cooker.'

'I thought you had actually invented it yourself,' I said.

'No, Watson. I have no objection to any improvement in the supply of hot chestnuts and potatoes on the winter streets, but I am prepared to leave the problems of the worker's diet to Baroness Coutts.'

We finished our simple meal in companionable silence. While we did so a paper boy came into the bar and passed the landlord the afternoon edition of the local evening paper. Mine host brought it with him when he fetched our next order of drinks.

'I don't know if you're sporting gents,' he said, 'but I thought you might wish a sight of the evening paper.'

I took it from him and thanked him, pleased at an opportunity to turn my thoughts away from Italian villainy and unlikely chestnut warmers. I had almost finished reading the sporting news and results when an item at the foot of the last page caught my eye.

'Great Heavens, Holmes!' I exclaimed. 'Something dreadful has happened in London!'

'How very informative,' he commented. 'Let me guess – Princess Alexandra has appeared in public in the same dress as the latest of the Prince's women?'

'No, Holmes,' I said. 'This is serious.' I read him the stop-press item that had caused my concern. 'Papal Secretary Attacked in London. Cardinal Tosca, Senior Cardinal Secretary to the Pope, has been found seriously injured in his hotel room in London. Scotland Yard says that foul play is indicated and an arrest is expected shortly.'

I looked at my friend. 'Is that not dreadful?' I said.

He drummed his long fingers on the table. 'It is certainly

very annoying,' he said, 'and will change my immediate plans. Are there no more details?'

I shook my head. 'No,' I said. 'Do you want to wait for the next edition?'

'By the time that appears we might be in London, provided that you drink up immediately.' He drew the battered watch from the pocket of his ill-kempt waistcoat. 'If we pedal hard we can just make Guildford in time for the next train.'

On the journey back to London Holmes was silent. I tried to draw from him a theory as to the cause of the attack on Cardinal Tosca, but either he had none or did not choose to discuss it with me. At the terminus he left our bicycles in the care of the railway company and strode outside to hail a cab.

I was surprised to find that we were returning to Baker Street. 'I had thought,' I ventured, 'that you would wish to see the scene of the crime while it is fresh.'

'Fresh!' he snorted. 'The paper says that Scotland Yard is involved, which means that, so far from being fresh, the scene will have been stampeded over by battalions of unseeing and unthinking constables, aided and abetted by so-called detectives. No, Watson, we shall return home and await Lestrade, who knows my interest in the Cardinal and will, no doubt, appear on our doorstep very soon. He is like you, not entirely unobservant, though like you he rarely understands the significance of his observations.'

He was evidently not in a good mood, so I remained silent while we travelled to our lodgings and after we arrived there.

It was about half an hour after our return that Mrs Hudson showed Lestrade in.

'Come in, come in,' said Holmes. 'Take the basket chair, Lestrade. Help yourself to a cheroot and tell us all about the assault on Cardinal Tosca.'

Lestrade rooted in the coal scuttle, seeking one of Holmes' cheroots, then dropped into the basket chair and lit it.

'Well,' he said, 'I see you are up with the news, Mr Holmes. And I thought I might be the first to tell you.'

'I know only what the newspapers had by lunch time,' Holmes replied, 'which is that the Cardinal has been found seriously injured, foul play is indicated and an arrest expected. Taking the first statement to be true, has the second statement any factual basis and is the last statement more than an attempt by your colleagues to set the public mind at rest?'

Lestrade drew on his cheroot while he unravelled my friend's questions in his mind. Evidently he concluded that discretion is the better part of valour and avoided argument by beginning a recitation of what he took to be the facts.

'His Eminence,' he began, 'as we all know, has been for some days at the Imperial Hotel, where he had a suite. He was accompanied in his suite by a young man, also of the clerical persuasion, a Father . . .' He faltered to a pause and consulted his pocketbook.

'Cioffi,' he said at last, mispronouncing the name dreadfully. 'That's it, Cioffi.' And he mispronounced it again, differently.

'While the Cardinal has been in London, he has received many visitors from among the Italians living here. Some of them were purely social and a lot were from people with problems who wanted the Cardinal to intervene with somebody or assist them in some way. Father, er . . . his assistant's job was to make his appointments and find out why people wished to see His Eminence. He was also supposed to weed out the folks that were a bit peculiar or downright barmy. As you will know, Mr Holmes, any person in public life attracts all sorts of people who aren't quite right.'

Holmes nodded. 'I am entirely familiar with the kind of thing that you mean,' he said.

'Well,' continued Lestrade, 'this morning a young man called to see the Cardinal. He said that he was from the same village as Cardinal Tosca, and that he needed the Cardinal's help. He had a paper with him, written in Italian.'

'What was it?' asked Holmes, sharply.

'It was a letter of introduction from someone in Sicily, recommending the young man to Cardinal Tosca's attention.

The young Father says that it seemed genuine and in order and that the young man was clean and civil, so he had no reason not to introduce him.'

'Did the youth give a name?' enquired Holmes.

'He did,' said the Inspector, and consulted his notes again. 'He called himself Luigi Pisciotto. The Father noted that name down and, when the Cardinal's previous visitor had left, he showed this Luigi Pisciotto into Cardinal Tosca's sitting room.'

'What time was that?' asked Holmes.

'That was about ten o'clock.'

'Was anyone else in the suite, apart from the Cardinal and Father Cioffi?'

Lestrade shook his head. 'No,' he said. 'The Cardinal saw his visitors alone and his assistant remained outside unless the Cardinal rang for him. In this case he did not ring and his assistant set about dealing with some letters for a while. After about half an hour he realized that the Cardinal's next visitor was about due, so he tapped the door, intending to remind him. He got no answer, so he tried again. Getting no reply a second time, he looked into the Cardinal's sitting room.'

'And what did he see?' asked my friend.

'The Cardinal was sprawled on the floor face down in a puddle of blood.'

'Was he seriously injured, as the newspapers suggest?'

'He was dead, Mr Holmes,' said Lestrade, and a near-smile flickered across his sallow features at the thought that for once he had trumped Sherlock Holmes.

Fourteen

An Arrest is Expected

'Dead!' exclaimed Sherlock Holmes. 'The papers said only that he was injured.'

'So they did,' agreed Lestrade, who was now evidently relishing his small triumph. 'It so happens that the Cardinal's next appointment was with George Morton, a penny-a-liner for the religious papers. He arrived at the Cardinal's suite just as the young Father called for assistance. Old George didn't waste time – he was off like a shot to sell his news. If he'd waited, he'd have had a bigger story, that the Pope's best pal had been murdered in London.'

'Go back to the point at which Cioffi entered the Cardinal's sitting room,' said Holmes, flicking an impatient forefinger. 'Can you describe the room? I take it that you have been there.'

'Oh, yes,' confirmed Lestrade. 'As my superiors at the Yard were aware of my interest in the Cardinal, they have put the case under my investigation. I would have consulted you, Mr Holmes, but the matter seems fairly straightforward and I do expect an arrest very soon.'

'Do not foreshadow your story,' said Holmes. 'You were about to describe the room.'

'Ah, yes. Well, it's a good, big room, with double doors from the outer room where the Cardinal's assistant had his desk. When you go in there's a door to the right that leads to the bedroom. The windows are opposite you, two of them. In front of the windows is a large desk, with a big chair behind it and three in front. There is a long couch along the left-hand wall and a big cabinet on the right, between the corner and the bedroom door.'

'Is there a way out through the bedroom?' asked Holmes.

'No, Mr Holmes. There's a bathroom that way, but no way out except by the double doors.'

'Where, then, was Luigi Pisciotto when Father Cioffi entered the room?'

Lestrade lost a little of his smugness. 'That is, indeed, a bit of a problem, Mr Holmes. He was not there.'

'You are sure of that?' demanded Holmes. 'Father Cioffi did not leave the room unattended when he went for help?'

'No, Mr Holmes. He went to his desk and rang for a page, sending him to fetch a doctor and the police. That's how Morton came to hear about it.'

'When Cioffi entered, where was the Cardinal lying and how was he injured?'

'As I said, the Cardinal was lying on the carpet, as though he'd pitched forward out of one of the armchairs in front of the desk. His feet were towards the right-hand end of the desk and his head inclined towards the door. He had been stabbed in the lower left of the, er . . . belly, the, er . . . sorry Doctor, abdomen. It was a deep, vicious wound and there were a couple of other stabs in the Cardinal's back and shoulders.'

'Do you know what was the weapon?'

'The surgeon says it was a long, narrow-bladed knife with a good point, but not very sharp on the edges.'

'And have you found the paperknife?'

Lestrade blinked. 'How did you know it was a paperknife, Mr Holmes?'

'Oh, come now, Lestrade. What you have described is a paperknife, and the murder took place immediately alongside the Cardinal's desk. I imagine that there was one on the desk, was there not?'

'There was, Mr Holmes, and it was found in Porter Lane.'

'Where,' concluded Holmes, triumphantly, 'the murderer dropped it after fleeing from the scene of the crime via the bathroom window and a convenient drainpipe.'

Lestrade was looking positively crestfallen, seeing his small advantage over my friend ebb away on the flow of Holmes' deductions.

'That's what we think, too,' he said, lamely.

'So,' Holmes went on, 'Cardinal Tosca was stabbed fatally while in his sitting room with Luigi Pisciotto, who apparently bore the Cardinal some malice.'

'Why do you say that, Holmes?' I interjected.

'The wounds to the back, Watson. A single and fatal stab wound might be the work of a hired assassin, but having killed his man, Luigi Pisciotto, if it was indeed him, inflicted extra wounds. They are the mark of his passion and malice.'

'But why do you say that it might not have been Pisciotto?' enquired the police detective, still mangling the unfamiliar name. 'There was nobody else in the room.'

'You said that Father Cioffi occupied the Cardinal's suite with him,' recalled Holmes. 'Where were his quarters in relation to those of Cardinal Tosca?'

'As you go in,' said Lestrade, 'there is a hallway, running from side to side. The doors to the assistant's office are straight in front of you and a single door on the right leads to his sleeping quarters and bathroom.'

'So it would be possible,' said Holmes, 'as I thought it might be, for the Cardinal to admit someone to the suite while his assistant was in his own quarters.'

'Ah,' exclaimed Lestrade. 'I see what you're driving at, Mr Holmes, but the Cardinal assistant had breakfast with him in the sitting room before he began work. There was nobody there then,' and he grinned, his spirits restored.

'Of course not,' said Holmes, impatiently. 'But there might have been someone in His Eminence's bedroom or bathroom, might there not?'

'What sort of person would the Cardinal admit in the middle of the night?' asked Lestrade, with an expression of genuine puzzlement.

'Great Heavens, Lestrade!' Holmes exclaimed. 'We may be discussing a prince of the Church, but we both know that he was a sexual invert who was not above availing himself of New York's boy houses!'

'But,' said Lestrade, rallying, 'if there had been another person in the Cardinal's room – other than himself and Pisciotto, that is – where has that person gone to?'

'You do not know where Pisciotto has gone to,' replied Holmes. 'You know only that he must have exited by the window of the bathroom. Might I remind you that what one person can do another may emulate?'

'We have a good description of Pisciotto,' said the little police officer. 'We shall have him in custody soon.'

'The Italian community is notoriously protective of its own,' commented Holmes.

'So they may be,' said Lestrade, 'but the Cardinal Archbishop has offered a handsome reward. Someone will know where he is and sell him to us.'

'And how will you frame your case against him?' asked Holmes, with apparent innocence.

'Very easily, I should think,' answered Lestrade, stoutly. 'Firstly, Father Cioffi says he would recognize him again, so he will identify Pisciotto as the man who went into the Cardinal's room last before he was killed. Secondly . . .' and he paused.

'Secondly?' Holmes prompted, but Lestrade remained silent. 'You have no witness to the deed,' continued Holmes, 'and a weapon which was taken from the Cardinal's own desk and cannot, therefore, be tied to Pisciotto. Do you have any idea of the motive behind the killing?'

'Well now, Mr Holmes, you and I both heard the American tell us about Cardinal Tosca's associations in New York and elsewhere. Evidently he has caused some offence or posed some threat to his former companions in crime and they sent this young man to gain an interview by a ruse and then kill the Cardinal.'

'Very good, Lestrade. A possibility, indeed, but one that is eliminated by the evidence.'

'How is that, Mr Holmes?'

'You have a young man whose only connection with the Cardinal was that they shared a birthplace, and who required a letter of introduction to give him access to the great man. So he is admitted to the Cardinal's presence, and what happens then, Lestrade?'

'Why, he waits his opportunity, then when it arises he seizes the paperknife and plunges it into His Eminence, making his escape through the bathroom.'

'And where was Tosca when the opportunity you spoke of arose?'

'From the way he was lying he must have been sitting in the right-hand armchair in front of his desk. It looked as though he had toppled forward out of that chair.'

'Precisely,' said Holmes. 'This great official of the Church, who has graciously granted a few minutes of his time to an unknown young man, is not sitting behind his desk, conducting a formal conversation, but has come around the desk and sat with his visitor in close informality. In which position, this assassin, having brought no weapon with him, strikes a blow with the convenient paperknife and so far forgets that he is a cold-blooded murderer as to strike further blows in hot blood. If you propose to argue that Pisciotto is an agent of some Italian secret society, you will need a better story than that.'

'Well, there may be weaknesses that we shall have to look into, Mr Holmes, but the Crown does not have to prove a motive in any case.'

'Indeed not,' agreed Holmes, 'but you are in a particular difficulty in this matter.'

'What difficulty do you see, Mr Holmes?'

'If Pisciotto is caught and brought to trial, the Crown can present a theory that the murder was the work of a secret society bent on destroying His Eminence as one of the organization's enemies. If his defence is a simple denial of guilt, that will suffice for the jury and the public and will earn you golden opinions from the Cardinal Archbishop and his master in Rome, but what if he pleads the so-called "Pompey Defence"?'

'The Pompey Defence?' repeated Lestrade, with a bewildered expression. 'I think you have the advantage of me, Mr Holmes. I'm a Board School boy, with no classical education.'

Holmes smiled. 'I was not referring to the ancient Roman Pompey, but to the city which carries that nickname in the Royal Navy because of the erstwhile presence of a naval prison there – Portsmouth. You may know the manoeuvre as the 'Sailors' Defence' or by one of its other sobriquets.'

Lestrade still seemed puzzled and Holmes went on. 'I am talking about the plea – very common in seaports – that a young man has assaulted or killed an older man because the older man made an indecent suggestion to him or an assault upon him. If Pisciotto makes that plea, how will you disprove it?'

'We shall establish that he committed the murder, to the satisfaction of any jury,' said Lestrade, firmly, 'and that will be sufficient.'

'It will be sufficient,' remarked Holmes, 'to make the Cardinal Archbishop regret offering a reward and will not earn you the Pope's gratitude.' He shook his head. 'I do not see you acquiring a Papal Knighthood from the result of this case, Lestrade.'

Fifteen

A Nocturnal Excursion

The joust with Lestrade worked wonders on my friend's disposition so that at dinner he was an amiable companion – so much so that I ventured to raise the case again for there were certain questions that I had been nurturing.

'Holmes,' I said, 'do you really believe that Lestrade has got it all wrong?'

'Lestrade,' said Holmes, 'is among the best of the Scotland Yarders, and has no reason at all to be ashamed of his Board School education. He has done very well to reach his rank with his disadvantage of height, but he does have a certain tendency to adopt the most obvious explanation, however implausible it may be.'

'But I thought you said that the simplest explanation was usually the correct one!'

'Full marks, Watson! So I did – the simplest explanation, not necessarily the most obvious.'

'So,' I said, 'do you really believe that there was another person present in Cardinal Tosca's suite?'

He shook his head. 'It is extremely unlikely,' he admitted. 'I was simply twitting Lestrade, who had never considered the possibility and had, consequently, taken no steps to see if it had happened.'

'Then you believe that this Luigi Pisciotto is the killer?'

'Unless something very singular has occurred, that seems the simplest explanation, and the simplest explanation, as I have just observed, is usually the correct one.'

I had one more question. 'When we first knew that the

95

Cardinal had been attacked, you said something about it altering your plans. I imagine that is even more true now that Cardinal Tosca is dead.'

'Indubitably,' he said. 'It had been my intention to follow friend Petrosino's line and to continue to bring pressure to bear on the Cardinal while he negotiated with Corese. That way, I believed that he would, in the end, sell out his fellow conspirators.'

'What will you do now?' I asked.

He frowned. 'I might have persuaded Tosca to give me the names of Father Grant's murderers, but I shall certainly not be able to persuade Corese. So far as the killers are concerned, I shall have to devise another method of unearthing their identity. In the meantime I shall do my best to secure the Vatican Cameos.'

'But you believe that they are in Corese's safe!' I exclaimed.

'Precisely,' he agreed.

'But surely you are not going to attempt to take them from his safe, Holmes?'

'You seem to lack confidence in my criminous skills, Watson. I should have thought that you had accompanied me on enough nefarious adventures to have convinced you that I know what I am about with a jemmy and dark lantern.'

'This is not a joking matter,' I said, sternly. 'You know from Petrosino the nature of the man Corese, that he will kill without a thought. You cannot risk yourself in such a venture.'

'Watson,' he said, 'your concern for my safety touches me as always, but you know very well that I have chosen a profession in which physical risk must sometimes be accepted and that, when it arises, I do accept it.'

'But the place will be guarded!' I protested.

'It was not so this morning, nor is there any reason why it should be. Corese is not in New York, surrounded by his enemies and competitors and sought by the police. He is in the English countryside, where he believes that nobody knows his true identity and that he is not wanted by the police. To set up any consequential guard system would simply draw unwelcome attention to him. No, Watson, I believe that we shall have a relatively simple task ahead of us.'

'"We",' I repeated. 'So you wish me to accompany you?'

He inclined his head. 'I had hoped for your valuable and comforting assistance, Watson, but I would not, of course, blame you for refusing. We will, after all, be breaking the law.'

'Hang breaking the law!' I exclaimed. 'I am more concerned with your safety, Holmes, and you know perfectly well that if you wish me to accompany you I shall be proud to do so.'

'Thank you, Watson. You are a good friend.'

I have to record that, despite my forebodings about his plan, his simple words warmed my heart.

'When shall we go?' I asked.

'Tomorrow night will not be too soon,' he replied. 'If I thought that your calf muscles could stand the journey twice in one day, I might go tonight, but I think tomorrow will do.'

So it was that we strapped our bicycles to the back of a cab and set out the next evening to catch a late train to Guildford. Our journey was uneventful and, once an initial stiffness had been overcome, I was pleased to see that I found it easier to keep up with Holmes' pedalling pace.

We did not risk a call at the little wayside inn, though I passed it with a regretful glance. A little further on Holmes called softly, 'Watson, I think we should douse the acetylene lamps. We know the road and there is no danger of collision. Better not to draw attention to ourselves.'

We extinguished our lamps and rode in silence until we reached Corese's villa. The surrounding mass of trees was black in the gloom, but the ornate gate still stood open beneath them.

We dismounted from our machines at the gate and leaned them against a tree trunk just inside. Holmes carefully checked his pockets and his saddle-bag to ensure that he had the necessary tools for our expedition, then lit a small dark lantern and closed its slide before handing it to me.

'Now,' he hissed, 'the game's afoot, Watson,' and even in the deep shadow of the trees I thought I could detect the trace of a grin on his pale features.

We made our way stealthily along the drive, walking on the grass. We were coming close to the house when Holmes reached out a restraining hand and halted me. He pointed to a particularly large tree ahead and indicated in dumb show that I should listen.

A slight night breeze was moving the branches above us, so that there was a constant rustling, but after a few moments of straining my ears I believed that I could hear another sound against the sussuration of the trees. I mimed sleep to Holmes and he raised a thumb. He agreed that something – a large animal or a human being – was dozing on the other side of the tree.

Holmes indicated that I should stay where I was, then he drew a blackjack from his coat pocket and stepped quickly around the tree trunk. A second later I heard the soft thud of his weapon, followed by the sound of someone tumbling to the grass and Holmes' whispered, 'Watson!'

I joined him quickly, where he stood with a sprawled body at his feet. 'Give us some light,' he commanded as he rolled his victim over.

Cautiously opening the lantern's slide, I could see that the figure was that of a muscular young man, dressed in sailor's canvas slops, though he wore the decorated belt of a London hooligan. Holmes rifled the man's pockets and came up with a handful of papers which he held under the lantern.

'Sailor's papers in the name of Murphy,' he commented as he replaced them. 'I do not think he is a guard for Corese. I fear we may have been forestalled. Douse the glim, Watson. If we are to do any good here we shall need to be quick about it.'

We continued towards the house until it came in sight through the trees. I was heartened to note that no window showed the least light. Unless there were people awake at the rear it looked as if the entire household was asleep.

Once again Holmes restrained me. 'Hold hard, Watson!' he whispered. 'There is something very wrong here.'

'What do you mean?' I whispered back. 'All the lights are off.'

'So they are,' he agreed, 'but the second window along the side of the ground floor is open. If you owned a collection like Corese's, would you leave a ground-floor window open?'

I followed his pointing finger and was still staring at the black opening when a light sprang up in a window to the rear of the open one. A moment later a muffled cry came from inside the house.

'Quick, Watson!' Holmes hissed. 'Back to the bicycles! We must be ready to beat a hasty retreat.'

We slid through the trees, passing our unconscious sailor, and regained the tree by the entrance where our machines waited. Behind us more lights had sprung up in the house. I was mounting my cycle when Holmes stopped me.

'We do not need to leave just yet,' he observed. 'I would like to await events a little longer.'

A distant sound of breaking glass reached us and was soon followed by running footsteps approaching through the trees.

'If he comes this way, Watson, stop him at all costs!' hissed Holmes and drew me against a tree.

The footsteps were almost upon us when we stepped from under the tree. I caught a glimpse of a tall figure in black, then Holmes' arm went up with the blackjack in his fist and the runner crumpled under a well-aimed blow.

'Quick, Watson,' Holmes commanded. 'We cannot leave him on Corese's ground. Let me fling him across your crossbar and we will wheel him a little distance.'

'But won't they follow from the house?' I asked.

'No. They have already found the sailor Murphy. It will take them a little while to work out that he is not the man they were chasing.'

With no little difficulty we laid the unconscious runner across the crossbar of my bicycle and we managed to push it some yards along the road. Eventually Holmes stopped us and we rolled our captive on to the roadside grass. Holmes rifled the man's pockets while I fetched the dark lantern. Its narrow beam revealed a face I had seen before – the long, pale features of the Reverend Mr Cravat.

'Well now,' remarked Holmes, 'that is something I had not expected.'

Sixteen

An Arrest is Made

I stood warily at the roadside, keeping an eye on Corese's premises, while Holmes examined Cravat's clothing, showing me a dark lantern, jemmy and blackjack which he found in the Reverend gentleman's pockets.

'What shall we do with him?' I asked, as Holmes straightened up.

'Nothing,' he said. 'I suggest that we make him comfortable here on the grass and leave him to sleep the sleep of the unjust. Corese's people, if I judged the distant noises accurately, have found the man Murphy. They will assume that he was a lone opportunist burglar who stunned himself in an encounter with a tree in the dark. There is nothing about his person that has been taken from the villa, so they will let him go.'

'What if they call the police?' I asked.

He chuckled. 'I do not think that Signor Benetti alias Corese would welcome any police interest in his affairs. No, Watson, there has been an unsuccessful attempt at burglary and Corese will let it end there, though I imagine that young Mr Murphy will suffer a little at the hands of Corese's minions before he is turned loose.'

We left Cravat comfortably disposed at the side of the road and mounted our bicycles. Holmes, despite the failure of his plan, seemed to be in an astonishingly amiable mood and was humming to himself.

'You sound cheerful,' I remarked, as we pedalled away.

'I was thinking,' he said, 'that there are elements of this affair that will tickle Petrosino's musical sense of humour.

101

Sailors taking to housebreaking has a certain smack of *The Pirates of Penzance* about it, don't you think?' and he began to sing softly:

> 'Come friends who plough the seas,
> Truce to navigation, take another station,
> Let's marry piracy with a little burglary.'

'And where,' I enquired, matching his mood, 'does Mr Cravat fit into the picture?'

'Ah! There you have me, Watson. Perhaps he is that "Doctor of Divinity who is located in this vicinity" who is mentioned in the operetta but never appears. Still, it gives me some moral comfort to know that I am not the only amateur cracksman who ventures out at night with dark lantern, jemmy and blackjack, and that burglary is a suitable pastime for the clergy. It rather reminds one of those robust old country parsons who used to be devoted to the hunting field.'

'To be serious,' I said, 'why do you think Cravat was at Corese's villa?'

'That is obvious, Watson – to lay his hands on the Vatican Cameos, what else? He will have reasoned as I did, that the death of Cardinal Tosca has made it impossible to get at the Cameos through him and that pre-emptive action was necessary.'

'But how would he have known that Benetti is Corese and that the Cameos are in his safe?'

'Probably by having me watched,' he said, unruffled. 'He has plenty of adherents of his dubious cause in London.'

'What will you do about the Cameos now?' I enquired, imagining that there would be a further expedition in the near future.

'Corese,' he said, 'will take additional precautions for at least a little while. Since he has not got Cravat, merely a sailor hooligan, he will probably not realize that the attempt was aimed at the Vatican Cameos, but he will wish to protect his collections. I think that we may safely let the Cameos rest where they are for the time being.'

We reached Guildford and travelled back to London by a milk train, slipping into 221b Baker Street in the small hours of the morning.

I was late down to breakfast and Holmes was before me. Hardly had I joined him at the table when Mrs Hudson announced Lestrade.

'Bring him in, Mrs Hudson, bring him in,' said Holmes, 'and set another place. If he has worked last night he will welcome a good breakfast.'

The little policeman was pleased to accept Holmes' hospitality and tucked in vigorously, Holmes preventing any discussion until we had all eaten.

At last Lestrade laid down his napkin. 'I told you, Mr Holmes, that an arrest would be made, and it has been.'

'You have Pisciotto in custody?'

'So we do, and I have the American detective to thank. He tipped us off that a youth had arrived at Mrs Ruggiero's yesterday who matched the description of the wanted man, so last night we went along and arrested both of them.'

'You arrested Petrosino?' I exclaimed.

'I did,' he agreed. 'Firstly because it helps his pose if he is treated as a suspect by the police, and secondly because he knocked me down the first time we met.'

We all chuckled. 'Never fear,' he went on, 'I have just released him, but young Pisciotto has been charged with the murder of Cardinal Tosca.'

'And is he the right man?' enquired Holmes, innocently.

'Of course he is,' said the Inspector. 'The Cardinal's assistant has identified him as the young man who came with the letter of introduction. He is quite sure about that. That's all I need.'

'Where is the letter of introduction?' asked my friend.

'We don't have it,' admitted Lestrade. 'The Cardinal's assistant gave it back to Pisciotto, to show to the Cardinal. It was not in the murder room and Pisciotto didn't have it when we arrested him. But it's of no great moment, is it?'

'No, perhaps not,' Holmes agreed. 'I was merely thinking that it would enable a check to be made on his antecedents.

103

If he is, as you suspect, an instrument of Corese's Rule of Nine, he is likely to have operated under an alias and may be wanted elsewhere for other matters.'

'He was using a false name, that's true, but not entirely false. He says his name is Angelo Pisciotto, not Luigi.'

Holmes' eyes opened wide. 'How very singular!' he exclaimed.

'Singular, Mr Holmes?' said the Scotland Yard man. 'How's that?'

'That a hired killer should arrive at his victim's door with a letter of introduction that identifies him by a slight variant of his real name, that he should be carrying no weapon, and that he should be willing to commit murder in a room from which the only exits were past a witness who had already seen him or down three floors of drainpipe. It is a very singular set of circumstances.'

The Inspector looked sharply at Holmes, as though to judge if his leg was being pulled, but Holmes' face was entirely serious.

'With all due respect, Mr Holmes, it is you who talks about the simplest solution being best, but here you are making complications where none really exist. Angelo Pisciotto has been identified by the young Father as the man he admitted to the Cardinal's sitting room – he is quite sure of that. What's more, there's staff of the hotel who say that Pisciotto was waiting early in the morning. It won't matter if he's wanted elsewhere, Mr Holmes. He is going to hang in London.'

'And the man himself,' said Holmes, 'what does he say? Has he admitted it?'

'He admits he was at the hotel early in the morning, but he will not say why. He says he did go there to see the Cardinal, but he won't tell us what his business was and he won't explain why, if he'd gone there to speak to Cardinal Tosca, he didn't go upstairs.'

'When he was arrested,' said Holmes, 'was he wearing the clothes in which he went to the hotel?'

'So far as Father Cioffi can recall, yes. It's difficult,

because all these Italian fellows dress alike, but Father Cioffi thinks he was.'

'And was he very badly bloodstained?' asked Holmes.

'No, Mr Holmes. There was no trace of blood on his clothing.'

To my surprise, Holmes changed the subject and, shortly afterwards, Lestrade left us.

'Holmes,' I said, when we were alone again, 'what was your point about bloodstains?'

'You are a doctor, Watson. If you plunge a large knife into someone's lower abdomen, inflict a fatal wound and then withdraw the knife, what happens?'

'Well, you will get a sudden release of the pressure in the circulatory system, so that initially blood will spurt and splash from the wound.'

'Precisely, Watson. So that the killer can hardly have failed to receive bloodstains on his hand and sleeve, if nowhere else. However, we do not need to theorize. We know that the murderer was bloodstained.'

'Do we?' I said. 'How do we know that?'

'Because of the way in which he left the Cardinal's suite. Father Cioffi, at his desk by the Cardinal's door, heard nothing to make him suspicious. Tosca did not cry out or ring for assistance. Whoever killed him had done so without making any untoward noise. If he was not significantly bloodstained, he could have walked out of the Cardinal's sitting room and closed the door behind him. Cioffi would have been quite unsuspicious and unaware of the Cardinal's death until he showed in Tosca's next visitor.'

'Then you believe that Lestrade has the wrong man?'

'I do, Watson, but what has happened here in reality is still not clear to me, and what it might have to do with the Vatican Cameos, if anything, does not reveal itself to me. I suspect that we have drifted into very deep waters, my friend.'

Seventeen

Visitors to Baker Street

W e were not left long to contemplate the mystery before Mrs Hudson announced a caller. To my surprise, but not, apparently, to my friend's, it was none other than Commendatore Lindt.

Holmes greeted the Swiss officer frostily and motioned him to a chair. I noted his manner and the lack of any offer of hospitality. Holmes was the most generous of men and always concerned to set visitors at ease. I knew that his resentment was deep-seated and that he would neither forgive nor forget Lindt's crude attempt to use him as a hired assassin.

'What,' demanded Sherlock Holmes, 'have you come to request on this occasion?' and his eyes smouldered.

Lindt gave a little nervous cough, embarrassed perhaps, though whether by the frigid reception or his proposed errand I did not know.

'I think you misunderstood me on the last occasion I called,' he began.

'And I thought,' interjected Holmes, 'that I had understood you all too plainly, but please explain your present visit.'

'You cannot be unaware,' said Lindt, 'that the situation has now changed.'

'In what way?' demanded Holmes.

'Why, by the murder of Cardinal Tosca, of course.'

'The murder of the Cardinal merely adds a new confusion to the case,' said Holmes. 'The basic problems remain. You do not have the Vatican Cameos and I do not have the murderers of Father Grant. In addition, Scotland Yard has arrested and charged a man with the murder of Tosca.'

'That is hardly a problem,' said Lindt. 'I understand from the officer in charge of the case that it will be stated that the boy killed His Eminence on behalf of some secret society.'

'And what if the accused man says differently?'

'I had believed that accused persons are not permitted to give evidence in British Courts.'

'That is correct,' agreed Holmes, 'but he will undoubtedly be assigned a defending advocate, who will have a duty to cross-examine the Crown's witnesses on the basis of his client's allegations. You cannot prevent that, nor can you prevent the press reporting what is said in Court.'

'We are, as you say, jumping fences before we come to them, Mr Holmes. The accused man may yet confess.'

'He may,' said Holmes, 'but I would not bank on it. If Scotland Yard were going to obtain a confession, they would have had it by now.'

'Then we must deal with the trial when it happens,' said Lindt. 'In the meantime it occurs to me that the basis of our misunderstanding last time can now be avoided.'

'In what way?' demanded Holmes again.

'My concern is with the Vatican Cameos, yours is with bringing the killers of Father Grant to justice, yes?'

Holmes nodded but said nothing.

'I propose that we let the case of the late Cardinal take its course, and that we join forces to achieve our two objectives – to restore the Cameos to their rightful owners and to bring the killers to book.'

Holmes shook his head, slowly but emphatically. Uncoiling himself from his chair he stood and took a pipe from the mantelpiece.

'I do not think so,' he said. 'I believe that I might find the waters further muddied, were I to accept your proposal. Instead I will make a suggestion of my own. I know where the Vatican Cameos are and they are safe. Leave me to find the murderers and when I have done so I shall see that the Cameos reach Rome.'

'You know where they are?' said Lindt, suddenly excited.

Holmes stooped to light a spill. 'It was not very difficult,' he remarked. 'Even that bumbling fanatic Cravat managed to find out where they were.'

'Cravat found out where they were?' exclaimed Lindt.

'He did,' confirmed Holmes. 'Though he has not succeeded in laying his hands on them. You had better prevent that. I understand it to be his intention to destroy them.'

Lindt stood up, suddenly. 'I see that we are never going to come to an agreement, Mr Holmes, which I regret. Time presses and I am afraid I must take my leave,' and in an instant he was gone.

Sherlock Holmes flung himself back into his chair and laughed aloud.

'I do not see what you find amusing,' I said. 'That man is insufferable!'

'I was thinking,' said Holmes, 'that Cravat and Lindt richly deserve each other, Watson. They are a pair of fanatical and immoral scoundrels. What a pleasure it would be to observe any confrontation between them. Besides which, I believe that I have diverted Lindt's attention and removed him from the field of our endeavours.'

We had scarcely settled ourselves when Mrs Hudson appeared again. 'There is a loud and unpleasant man downstairs,' she complained, 'who seems to be a clergyman and insists that he will see you whether you wish it or not,' and she handed Holmes a card.

My friend's eyes sparkled at the name on the card. 'Oh,' he replied, 'I would not miss seeing this gentleman for worlds. Pray show him up, Mrs Hudson!'

A moment later Cravat marched into our sitting room.

Two spots of bright colour burned in his long and pallid features and his eyes flashed as he stopped in front of Holmes and pointed at my friend.

'You, Holmes,' he said, 'are a conniving scoundrel!'

'Mr Cravat,' said Holmes, and his tone was silken-smooth, a tone which I knew boded ill to his listener, 'you have arrived at my home without any appointment or apology; you have insulted my landlady; now you stand in my sitting room and insult me. Can you give me any good reason why I should not give way to my baser instincts and fling you down the seventeen stairs outside, before kicking you out into Baker Street?'

Cravat's eyes bulged. 'You would not dare attack me, Holmes. I am armed with the strength of the Lord and you would regret it.'

Holmes smiled. 'If you try my patience only a little further, Cravat, you may test the degree to which the Lord protects idiotic and bigoted bullies. If you have something sensible to say, please get on with it.'

The self-styled clergyman glowered at Holmes, his Adam's apple working in his scrawny neck. For a moment I thought that he might be fool enough to accept Holmes' challenge, but some glimmer of sense seems to have saved him.

'You were at Benetti's villa!' he accused.

'So I was,' agreed Holmes. 'But whereas I was there as an observer, you, it seems, were attempting to steal the Vatican Cameos.'

'I,' declaimed Cravat, 'was about the Lord's work and you, Holmes, shanghaied me, as you well know.'

Holmes smiled again. 'It is encouraging to note that you are not entirely stupid, Cravat. Pray, what made you think that the Cameos were in Benetti's villa?'

Even Cravat was not immune to flattery. He laughed. 'Do you think I did not have the good Cardinal watched as soon as he came back to London? From watching him I found out about Benetti, and the more I discovered, the more it seemed likely that the Cameos were at the villa.'

Holmes applauded silently. 'Very well done,' he said, 'but there are a number of important things which you have not discovered. You would do well to listen to me and note what I say because what I say may save your worthless life.'

'Why should I listen to you, Holmes? You are nothing but a professional trickster in the pay of the Roman Whore! Anything you tell me will be only to mislead me, I am sure of that.'

'You may think what you wish, Cravat, but I would not have even your worthless blood on my hands unnecessarily. Let me warn you that the man you call Benetti is in fact a Sicilian criminal whose real name is Vito Corese. Even his notoriously criminous home island found him too much, whereupon he emigrated to New York and formed an organization called the "Rule of Nine". The activities of that gang – including virtually every crime – have made him a much wanted man in the United States. For that reason he hides in the Surrey countryside under an assumed name and has begun his villainies in England. You would do well to steer clear of him.'

Cravat smiled, as nasty an expression as any other I had seen on his face. 'If you think,' he said, 'that you can feed me chaff about Benetti, you have another think coming. Benetti, as you well know, is the nephew of the Benetti who runs the ice-cream-cart and barrel-organ business. It was from watching you and your man that I caught on to that connection, so perhaps I should be grateful.'

'I repeat,' said Holmes, 'that the younger Benetti is an impostor and a dangerous villain. What happened to your man Murphy at his hands?'

'He suffered a sound thrashing by Benetti's men,' said Cravat, 'which you also caused. But I have had Murphy's revenge – I have let him know that the organ-grinder Parselli is your fellow. That'll put paid to your games!'

Holmes' eyes blazed and he sprang at the Irishman, grappling him by the throat.

'You infernal, meddling imbecile!' he snarled. 'Do you know what you have done? Parselli is not my man, as you call him. He is an American police officer who came here to track a wanted murderer and establish a case for arresting him. Your petty vengeance may have cost a brave man his life!'

I was out of my chair only seconds after Holmes attacked Cravat, desperately seeking to stop him before he throttled the wretched man.

'Holmes! Holmes!' I cried, tearing at his hands as he squeezed relentlessly at Cravat's scrawny throat. 'Do not do this! Holmes! Calm yourself!'

As suddenly as the attack had started, it ended. My friend released his grip on the Irishman's throat and Cravat slumped to the floor. I was able to ignore him, as he was wheezing too loudly to have suffered any long-lasting harm, and pay my attentions to Holmes.

He stood, his hands on his hips, rigid but trembling slightly. His eyes were closed and his face as white as alabaster. I was deeply troubled. Though Holmes had abandoned the use of cocaine since his return from the East, I wondered whether the scene I had witnessed was not an indication of renewed use or, worse, a symptom of long-standing damage done by the drug. After a long interval he opened his eyes and looked down at Cravat, who had crawled into a chair.

'Be a good fellow, Watson, and take that fool away before I go for him again.'

I heaved a sigh of relief, realizing that Holmes' outburst had been an explosion of his contempt for Cravat and his anger at the threat to Petrosino posed by the Irishman's actions. I did as I was bid and ushered Cravat from the room, returning to find Sherlock Holmes seated with his head between his hands.

'I am sorry, Watson,' he said as I re-entered the room, 'but that idiot may well have condemned poor Petrosino to a dreadful death. Now we must bend all our efforts to find him and save him from Corese.'

In the short time I had been gone from the room he had scribbled out two telegrams and now he rang for the boy, telling him that the wires must go immediately, reply paid, and that he must wait at the Post Office for any reply.

'Who are you telegraphing?' I enquired.

'The first is to my Irregulars,' he said. 'I have been

concerned for Petrosino's safety ever since we came across him, and I have tried to use the boys to keep an eye on him. Wherever he goes, they follow.'

'But how can you wire them?'

'Because they have established a command centre outside Lantern Street Post Office, where little Timmy Moon sits with a bag of bread and cheese and a supply of penny dreadfuls. Wherever the Irregulars follow Petrosino, they wire Timmy from any Post Office they pass and the postmistress at Lantern Street passes it on to him. In that fashion he is kept aware of Petrosino's approximate whereabouts all the time and a wire to him will tell us, hopefully within minutes.'

'And the second?' I asked.

'That was to Lestrade, advising him to warn all beat officers to arrest Petrosino on sight.'

'Our American friend will not be best pleased,' I suggested.

'Perhaps not, but he will be a great deal safer in the cells at Cannon Row than he is pushing a barrel organ about London's streets at present. Who knows what Corese's villains will do to him if they get their hands on him.'

'Is there anything else we can do, Holmes?' I asked.

'Until we hear from Timmy Moon, no,' he said, 'except possess ourselves in patience and pray that Petrosino escapes the Rule of Nine.'

Eighteen

The Search for Petrosino

It can only have been minutes before a reply reached us, but the time dragged like hours. Sherlock Holmes could be as patient as a cat by a mousehole when it served his purpose, but he hated to be frustrated when he required action.

Now he paced up and down our little sitting room, picking up his pipe and putting it down again unlit, peering from the window into the street and endlessly checking his pocket watch against the mantel clock. I knew that to counsel calm would be of no avail, so I waited in silence.

At last we heard the footsteps of Mrs Hudson's page on the stair and Holmes leapt to the door and bounded out on to the landing to meet the boy. He returned clutching a telegram.

'I have sent the boy for a cab, Watson. Pull on your boots, we must be about our business!'

In a very few minutes we were in a hansom, heading east at an alarming speed.

'Where are we bound?' I asked Holmes.

'Timmy's telegram says that the boys and Petrosino were last reported from Bordon Street in Deptford some forty minutes ago. They cannot be very far away and if Petrosino is working his machine we shall have little difficulty in finding him.'

'And if he is not?'

'Then it will be a great deal more difficult,' Holmes said, shortly.

I fell silent and occupied myself with trying to maintain my seat while our cabby plunged headlong at times and at others dropped his horse's speed to a crawl. Our route took us through the busiest part of the City, where we were often delayed by the density of traffic. On such occasions, wherever he thought it possible, our driver would wheel into tiny side streets and lanes, often taking us through a network of alleys until he could find a moderately clear street ahead.

Apart from the fact that we seemed to be heading in a generally south-eastward direction, towards Deptford, our cabby's manoeuvres made it impossible for me to track our progress until I smelt the closeness of the Thames and realized that we were skirting the landward side of the Tower of London and making for Tower Bridge.

I hoped that we would not be delayed by the bridge opening to allow shipping to pass, but soon saw that the roadway was lowered and no ships were approaching. In a very short time we were on the south side of the river, racing east towards Deptford.

Holmes sat tensed and had made no remark for much of our journey, merely drumming his long fingers on the top of his stick. Suddenly he said, 'I could wish that Petrosino had not chosen to entertain the people of Deptford today.'

'Why is that?' I asked.

'Because,' he said, 'there is a large community of Italian migrants in Deptford, the very people that Corese's organization preys on and terrorizes. Whatever the Rule of Nine may do in that area they are on home turf and may expect no one to interfere or offer evidence.

We were now among the streets of Deptford, a mixture of dockside commerce and slum dwellings and now our driver was exercised in avoiding great drays and wagons lumbering away, loaded or empty, from the riverside quays at Rotherhithe. Holmes told the cabby to make for Bordon Street and soon we were swinging around its corner, right alongside a little Post Office.

A shrill voice hailed us urgently and a ragged boy leapt into our path, narrowly escaping destruction under our horse's hooves.

'Pull up!' Holmes commanded the cabby and, when we did so, the lad raced from behind us. I recognized him as one of the Baker Street Irregulars.

'Mr Holmes,' the boy panted. 'Are you a-looking for the organ-grinder?'

'Certainly,' said Holmes. 'It is most urgent that we find him. Where is he? Timmy's wire said that he was at Bordon Street a short time ago.'

'So he was,' said the boy, 'and it was me what wired to Timmy while the others followed him, but when I caught them up they'd lost sight of him.'

'Where was that?' demanded Holmes.

'In Bullet Street, or thereabouts. They didn't want him to think as we was following him, so when he turned the corner they hung back. Then they went around the corner and he was gone, like he'd just vanished.'

'Have you seen his barrel organ?' asked my friend.

'Funny you should ask that, Mr Holmes. We had a look all about Bullet Street, but we couldn't see him, but we did find his hurdy-gurdy. It was pushed right up a little alley off of Crows Lane, one of them little walks what goes down towards the river.'

Holmes cast me a meaningful glance. 'Quickly!' he said to our informant. 'Jump up on the step and take us there!'

The boy did as he was told and we set off again. In minutes he brought us to a halt in a street close to the river. The buildings around were a mixture of warehouses and residences, but many of both seemed to have been boarded up for some time.

We disembarked and Holmes sent the boy back to Bordon Street Post Office with our cab, to wire both Timmy Moon and Lestrade and await a reply from the Inspector. As the vehicle rattled away we stood on the muddy pavement and peered into the narrow alley which had been indicated to us.

'This is worse than we thought,' I observed. 'There aren't even any witnesses here to turn a blind eye. A man could do as he pleases here.'

'Indeed,' said Holmes, and was moving into the little alley when a board broke behind us with a noise like a pistol shot.

We spun around to see a grubby hand lifting a board on one of the derelict houses from the inside. A moment later it was replaced by a grubby face and, one after another, half a dozen of the Irregulars slid out of the building and dropped to the street.

'Mr Holmes,' said their leader, 'have you seen Mikey? We sent him to telegraph you.'

'I have,' said Holmes, 'and I have sent him back to wire for reinforcements. He told me what happened here. What have you been doing?'

'Well, guv'nor, when we saw as the organ-grinder had vanished, we looked about for his hurdy-gurdy and like Mikey told you we found it up this alley. We couldn't see any sign of the Italian cove about, so we been searching through all these old houses and that. We was here pretty quickly after he disappeared, Mr Holmes, and we didn't see no cabs or wagons, so we reckoned he's got to be somewhere hereabouts.'

'Well done,' said Holmes. 'Which buildings have you searched?'

A number of houses were pointed out to us. 'To tell truth, guv'nor, we did the houses because they're small. We didn't fancy doing the warehouses and that. Some of them places are really big and dark and some on us was a bit frightened like.'

'Don't worry,' said Holmes. 'You have done very well, but now we must complete the search of this area. First, there is a chandler's in the street we just came through. Run there and fetch a pound of candles so that we do not have to work in darkness,' and he pressed a coin into the boy's hand.

Very soon we were all equipped with candles and Holmes sent the boys off in three groups to continue their search. He and I advanced on a derelict warehouse immediately alongside the fetid alley where Petrosino's organ stood.

Before entering the building, Holmes examined with care

116

the abandoned instrument, running his lens over parts of it. At last he straightened from his inspection.

'There are no signs of recent damage,' he said, 'and no bloodstains, but observe this.'

He passed me his lens and held his candle close for me, pointing to the handle of the instrument.

As soon as the lens focused I could see what he meant. A very small mark on the handle was revealed by the lens to be the four-stroked grid of the Rule of Nine.

'Do you think Petrosino did this?' I asked.

'It was certainly done recently,' he replied. 'There are fresh flakes of paint in the scratches. The handle has not turned and the instrument has not moved far since that was scratched. Petrosino cannot have been working in this unpopulated area, he can only have been pushing his instrument through on his way elsewhere. He must have turned a corner and realized, too late, that he had been ambushed. With considerable presence of mind he realized that his ambushers would not take the organ, so he left us a message. I am afraid that our worst forebodings have come true – he has been taken by Corese's thugs.'

I looked around me, at the dark, eyeless buildings and the dirty narrow street.

'He could be anywhere,' I said. 'He might be floating down the river at this very moment.'

'We must hope not, Watson. Here, assist me through this window if you would be so kind.'

The stench inside the abandoned warehouse was indescribable. Generations of tramps seemed to have used its ground floor as a temporary home, leaving all manner of detritus behind them. Despite the urgency of our quest, we had to look closely at every heap of waste paper or rags, every pile of bottles or rancid, rotting mattress, to be sure that it did not conceal our friend.

I do not know how long it took us to search every nook and cranny of the building's three floors, but at last we returned to the ground again.

'Now,' said Holmes, 'for the cellar.'

The mephitic reek which rolled out of the cellar when Holmes yanked open a door was sufficient to induce vomiting.

'Faugh!' I exclaimed. 'Do we really need to venture down there?'

'I'm afraid so, Watson, but I think a cigar is justified. It may provide some little distraction from the stench.'

'What is the smell?' I asked.

'Old London,' said Holmes, 'or rather her river. These old buildings are, in many cases, slipping into the Thames mud, which may have been why they are abandoned. Once the foundations have slid a little way, the tide starts to seep into the lower levels. What you can smell is the same ancient, poisoned river mud that reeks along the foreshores all the way down to the Estuary.'

Puffing vigorously on a cigar I followed him through the cellar door, not entirely certain that our candles would not ignite the stinking atmosphere about us.

Nineteen

A Deadly Trap

In the years of my association with my friend Sherlock Holmes I followed him into some very dangerous and unpleasant places, but few have left such a vivid impression on my memory as that noisome cellar in Deptford thirty years ago.

We were barely through the door before we were aware that this part of the building was much older than the structure above ground. The main floors were of brick, admittedly old and perhaps as much as two hundred years in age, but the walls of the cellar and the stairs were evidently of much greater age and made of stone.

We were forced to pick our way carefully, not just because we stepped by candlelight, but because the steps were slimed with mud and what appeared to be moss. Eventually we reached the cellar's floor and paused to take our bearings.

Our uplifted candles showed us that we stood in a kind of passageway, wide enough to permit the passage of bales of goods, no doubt, which stretched away from us into blackness. On either side the passage was flanked by a row of timber-built stalls, some with doors, some without. The smell, if possible, was a great deal worse than when we had entered the cellar door and beyond the reach of our candles' light we could hear the scuttle and slither of rats.

'I'm afraid,' remarked Holmes, 'that we will have to search each of these compartments. You take the right, Watson, and I will take the left.'

I was well aware of the urgency of our errand, but it was

difficult to make rapid progress. Every footfall was upon a surface that was yielding, slimy and treacherous, more like the bed of a stream than a floor. There were no windows in the whole cellar, so far as we could see, and, in some cases, the doors to the side stalls had to be smashed open, being padlocked to no apparent purpose, since they were all empty of anything except rubbish and rats.

Puffing furiously at our cigars, which did little to conceal the foul smell of the place, we moved through the cellar. As we went, I noticed that the floor sloped downwards and became more slimy and soggy the further we went.

I reached the far end ahead of Holmes, finding that there was, at the extreme end, a barred grating in the ceiling which admitted a little light. I called to Holmes to join me, for the combination of the light from the grating and my candle had shown me that there were fresh footprints in the ooze underfoot.

Holmes joined me rapidly, holding his own candle above the disturbed area of mud.

'You are right, Watson,' he said, after a minute or two. 'There has been either a dance or a struggle here and, having regard to the premises, a struggle is by far the more likely.'

He held his candle aloft and I did the same while we looked around us. In the far corner, against the end wall of the cellar, was a dark bundle of rags. Holmes made to probe it with his stick and I was turning away when my moving candle drew my attention to the jewelled gleam of red at the edge of the rags.

'Hold hard, Holmes!' I said. 'There's blood there!'

Together we approached the heap. A large rat, its eyes glinting in the candlelight, scurried away from behind the pile. Carefully we began to sift through the rubbish. At the top it was, as we had first believed, sodden rags of the kind that littered the entire cellar, but the removal of a very few revealed the bruised and bloodstained features of Detective Petrosino.

A mixture of relief and horror ran through me: relief at

finding the American and horror at the circumstances. Once I had checked his pulse, relief took control, for he was alive.

Holmes cleared the rubbish away from our unconscious friend as I examined Petrosino. He had evidently been beaten severely, about the body and the head and, apart from the bruises to his face, I detected indications that more than one rib was cracked and that his left leg was broken below the knee.

'We must get him to hospital as rapidly as possible,' I told Holmes once I had completed my examination.

'That will not be easy,' he said, and pointed with his stick.

I followed his indication and was appalled to note that Petrosino's unbroken leg was fettered at the ankle with a rusty iron ring, which was itself attached to a length of chain. As my eyes tracked the chain I realized that it was firmly attached to a great ring embedded in the wall of the cellar.

'Great Heavens, Holmes!' I exclaimed. 'They must have intended to keep the poor fellow here!'

'Not for very long, I fear,' replied Holmes.

He stepped under the barred grating and lifted his stick to rattle it against the bars. After a moment the head of one of the Irregulars appeared above us.

'Mr Holmes,' the boy said. 'Have you found him?'

'We have,' replied Holmes, 'and he is injured. What news is there of Inspector Lestrade?'

'He wired back to say as he was coming straightway, but he ain't got here yet.'

'Very well. See that I am told as soon as he does arrive. In the meantime, take the remainder of the telegram money and run to the chandler's for two coils of stout rope.'

'Right away, guv'nor!' the boy acknowledged and disappeared.

Holmes turned to me. 'It is going to be some time before we can get Petrosino into a hospital,' he said. 'How much can we do for him in the meantime?'

I cast a glance around the dark, filthy cellar. 'Not a great deal,' I said. 'However, since he has to be moved we should attempt to splint his leg and bind up his ribs. The problem is that we have nothing to work with.'

'Then we must improvise, Watson,' he said and, sliding out of his coat, began to remove his tie and pull his shirt over his head.

When he removed his shirt he passed it to me, along with his tie and his pocketknife. Quickly I began to try and splint Petrosino's injured leg, using strips of Holmes' shirt and fragments of one of the broken doors. Fortunately for my patient he remained unconscious throughout my crude ministrations. When his leg was as firmly protected as I could manage I turned my attention to his ribs and, with the help of more strips of shirt and my own waistcoat, succeeded in strapping and padding them in a fashion which I hoped would reduce movement, pain and further injury while the little American was removed from the cellar. From time to time as I worked I cast an eye on the rusting chain that held Petrosino firmly to the wall and wondered what proposal Holmes had for freeing my patient.

At last I straightened up. 'That's about the best I can do,' I told Holmes. 'Now, how are we going to get him out of here?'

Before he could reply we were hailed from above by an Irregular. 'Mr Holmes!' a voice cried. 'The bogies is here!' and a moment later we saw Lestrade's features appear at the grating above us.

'Mr Holmes?' he said. 'What's all this about? Have you got the American down there?'

'We have,' said Holmes. 'Corese's thugs have given him a severe beating. He has cracked ribs and a broken leg and maybe other injuries. We need to get him out quickly.'

'I've got a Sergeant and five Constables with me,' the Inspector replied. 'Do you want me to send them down to help?'

'They cannot help just now,' replied Holmes. 'Petrosino is

chained to the wall here. The first thing we must do is take that grating out. Have you a vehicle?'

'I've got a growler standing by.'

'Then see if you can hitch it to the grating and pull it out,' said Holmes. 'I sent one of the Irregulars for coils of rope. It should be possible.'

Soon we could hear Lestrade giving orders above and the sounds of the rope being secured to the grate.

'Holmes,' I said. 'Would it not be easier to obtain a hacksaw, cut through the chain and use the Constables to carry Petrosino carefully up the stairs?'

'Infinitely more easy,' he agreed, 'but time-consuming, and time is a luxury we do not possess. Have you not noticed that we are no longer standing in mud, Watson? We are standing in water, which means the tide is coming into the Thames and very soon, I believe, this cellar will be flooded.'

I had indeed failed to note the water that had crept in through the ancient stonework and was now steadily creeping up our boots. A quick glance around me showed what I had previously seen and failed to interpret – that the slimy growths on the walls ran all the way up to the ceiling. The incoming tide would flood the entire chamber.

'Great Heavens, Holmes!' I said. 'I wondered why they had left him alive. Now I see that they always intended that he should die by inches in this fearful place!'

'Precisely,' agreed Holmes. 'Now, do you think that, when a rope is available, we can tie Petrosino to one of the more complete doors?'

'You cannot float him,' I said. 'Not with the chain attached to him.'

'I do not propose to attempt that,' he said. 'But the water is rising faster and we must keep him out of it, if possible.'

Again we were interrupted from above. 'Stand clear!' someone shouted into the grating and we heard the snap of the cabby's whip. The rope on the bars tightened and a few small particles of dirt fell away, landing close to us, but the grating remained unmoved.

'Back up and pull again!' Lestrade's voice commanded. The whip cracked again and the rope tautened. More and larger debris showered down, and this time I thought that the grating budged a little.

Holmes and I watched from a safe distance as further attempts were made and, eventually, it became plain that the grating was moving a little. At last it gave way and clattered on to the ground above while parts of its stone seating broke away and fell into the cellar.

In a moment Lestrade appeared in the aperture above us.

'What now, Mr Holmes?'

'Drop us the ends of both ropes,' commanded Holmes, then turned to me. 'Drag that door over here, Watson. We must be very quick about this.'

For some minutes I had sensed the water rising about my feet, now it had reached my ankles and drenched my boots and I realized that we would be very lucky if we succeeded in releasing poor Petrosino from his prison before the tide filled the cellar.

Twenty

A Race Against Time

Once we had secured one of the broken doors, Holmes suggested that we tie the unconscious American to it as firmly as possible with the end of one of the ropes and we set about doing so with all the speed we could muster.

Our hands were now soaking wet and chilled, while the light from the aperture above us and the candle flames did little to illuminate our operation. Petrosino was still profoundly unconscious and I feared that he had been severely concussed or worse. Nevertheless, as we dragged him on to the rough boarding and began to lash him in place he emitted an occasional groan, which I took as a hopeful sign that he was not slipping away from us but might be gradually regaining consciousness.

At last we had him bound to the door. Lestrade had been observing our progress from overhead and Holmes now hailed him. 'Be ready to haul him free of the water!' he told the Inspector.

'But Holmes!' I protested. 'The chain will drag at his leg if Lestrade hauls him up!'

'That,' said Holmes, 'is the primary purpose of the second rope,' and, illustrating his comment, he quickly bent the second rope to the chain that held Petrosino.

'Now,' he called to Lestrade, 'have your fellows pull steadily on both ropes at once. Don't let Petrosino's leg take the weight of the chain. When you've got him as far above water as you can, secure the ropes.'

Willing hands soon took the ropes above and Petrosino was

125

lifted until he hung like a great doll on the side of the door, with the chain looped up alongside him.

'Well done, Lestrade!' called Holmes. 'There is a smithy in the next street. Go and requisition two stout hacksaws and I will do what I can with this chain.'

The little detective was off like a shot and Holmes turned to me, sniffing the air. 'At least the river water has reduced the reek in this place,' he remarked. 'Now we have only the immemorial reek of Old Thames to cope with. Nevertheless, I suggest another cigar unless my vesta case has been swamped.'

The water was now about our waists, but Holmes produced a cigar case and vestas from the pocket of his coat and we lit up. Hardly had we done so when Lestrade reappeared and lowered two hacksaws on a length of twine.

'Now, Watson,' said my friend. 'Once Petrosino is freed, he will need your attentions above, so I suggest that you make your way out and join Lestrade.'

'Holmes!' I protested. 'I cannot leave you alone down here!'

'There is nothing else that you may sensibly do,' he said, already laying a saw blade to a link of the chain.

'But,' I said, eyeing the swirling brown water which was entering the cellar at an increasing rate, 'how will you get out when you have freed Petrosino?'

'That,' he said, sawing away earnestly, 'is the secondary purpose of the second rope, Watson. I doubt if I shall have time to reach the stairs, but you may do so if you leave now.'

I saw that it was useless to argue with him and, despite my misgivings, left his side and began to push my way through the dark, foaming water towards the cellar stairs. The journey seemed endless as each step was a battle against water which now reached my chest, but at last I was stumbling up the cellar stairs.

I soon located the window by which Holmes and I had entered the building and clambered out, stumbling around the side to reach the riverside. There I found a narrow, cobbled jetty, its waterside held by a row of ancient and rotten stakes which groaned and shifted with every swirl of the inrushing tide. Lestrade lay sprawled on the cobbles, watching Holmes' efforts below, while the police officers and the Irregulars also formed an anxious audience about the hole in the ground. I was pleased to note that beyond them waited a horse-drawn ambulance.

At the sound of my squelching footsteps Lestrade looked up. 'My word, Doctor,' he said, 'you look fairly done in. Is there no way we can help Mr Holmes? The way that water's coming in has me worried.'

I shook my head. 'If he can put his blade through one link of that chain we can have Petrosino out in a twinkling of an eye and Holmes can come up on the other rope,' I said.

'I know that's his plan,' said the detective, 'but he's almost floating already and he hasn't got halfway through the chain.'

He pulled me down alongside him and I peered into the gloom below. The water had advanced a good deal since I had struggled out and Holmes was, indeed, barely keeping his footing as the brown tide foamed and swirled among the wrecked cubicles in the cellar. Still he clung grimly to the chain with one hand and sawed away at it with the other, though the movement of the chain and his own disturbance by the water meant that he could only apply two or three strokes before the saw jumped and he had to replace it in its cut. My fears for my friend deepened.

Suddenly a greater volume of water seemed to surge around Holmes, depriving him entirely of any foothold and leaving him clutching desperately at the chain and rope. When it subsided a little, he returned to his attack on the iron link, but he was now completely without any support. Nevertheless, he eventually succeeded in driving the hacksaw's blade through one side of the link.

I realized that he had only completed half the task and that his circumstances were growing both more difficult and more dangerous by the minute. I tried to estimate how long it had taken him to sever that first arm of the link and how much longer it would take him to cut the second. I do not know if my estimates were anywhere near correct, but when, having made them, I looked at the level of water below and the rate at which it was rising, I realized that Holmes would never be able to free Petrosino with the hacksaw.

'Give it up, Holmes!' I shouted to him. 'You cannot cut the link in time. The water will rise too far. Climb up the second rope and let one of us hang down and cut the chain!'

He glanced upwards long enough to emit a terse, 'Nonsense!' then reapplied himself to his task, but a few more cuts at the iron must have shown him the hopelessness of his task. He tied the hacksaw to the twine with which it had been lowered and, relinquishing his left hand's grip on the chain, took the partly severed link between both his hands.

At first I did not understand his intention, but then I realized that he was proposing to force open the cut he had made to the extent that would enable him to slip a link free through the gap.

I have long known that Holmes is a man who never takes exercise for its own sake, but early in our acquaintance I realized that his long, lean frame concealed a considerable strength. I have recorded elsewhere, for example, an occasion when he straightened between both hands an iron poker that had been bent double and barely drew a long breath after doing so. Nevertheless I believed that his efforts to force the iron link open would fail, if not because of the link's inherent strength, then because he had no foothold and nowhere against which he could brace himself to apply leverage.

Lestrade and I watched in silence as Holmes wrestled with the iron, unable to see among the swirling foam if he was having any success.

Barely had Lestrade muttered, 'He'll never do it, Doctor. He's a game 'un, but he'll never do it,' when a noise like the report of a pistol sounded beneath us and the chain fell away, leaving only a couple of links still attached to Petrosino.

'Quickly!' I commanded Lestrade. 'Get your colleague up on the rope and let us assist Holmes!'

The party of policemen soon had control of the rope that held Petrosino suspended, and drew him easily and carefully over the edge of the hole. As soon as he was clear, we freed him from the rope and he was rushed to the ambulance and taken away rapidly.

With the American as safe as we could make him, my concern for Holmes returned. I ran back to the edge of the hole and peered down. There was no sign of him. I sprawled at length on the muddy cobbles and tried to look further into the cellar, but all I could see was the swirling brown tide, rising ever closer to the ceiling, and an occasional frightened rat swimming by and being sucked under. The second rope hung empty.

'Holmes!' I shouted at the top of my lungs. 'Holmes! Where are you?'

Lestrade ran up. 'Lestrade!' I cried. 'Holmes is lost somewhere in this filthy pit!'

You must bear in mind that, at this time, it was barely a year since Sherlock Holmes had returned from the three years' absence following his disappearance in Switzerland, during which time I had believed him to be dead. It flashed through my mind as I sprawled beside a hole in the pavement in Deptford that I had a thousand times rather that my friend had met his death in the roaring white torrent of the Reichenbach Falls than that he should be sucked down by the Thames into some corner of the rotting hold below me, only to be found when the reeking waters retreated.

I do not know now, and I certainly did not know then, what it was that I believed I might do to save my friend, but I sprang up and, without further thought, seized the second rope and began to slither down it into the cellar.

Hardly had I begun to move down the slippery, twisting rope, when two shapes hurtled past me, emitting shrill cries as they fell. They struck the water below and disappeared, while I clung to the rope and wondered. Two seconds later there emerged from the brown tide the cropped heads of two of the Irregulars, the same two who had kept watch at the bakery and with whom Holmes and I had shared tea and buns. I was moved by their loyalty to Holmes but fearful that they would be swept away as Holmes had been, and lose their own young lives in their attempt to assist him.

In a moment I could see that I was wrong. One of them seized the foot of the rope to which I clung and, with his other hand, grasped his comrade's hand firmly. The second pivoted about his friend, forming a sort of rotating sweep about the bottom of the rope.

As I continued my descent I heard one of them call out, 'There he is! There's Mr Holmes!' and looked down to see if they were right.

Sure enough, at the extreme edge of the area of light there had come into sight a floating chunk of board, beyond which could be seen what looked like Holmes' head. The outermost youth reached desperately for the timber, almost breaking his hold on his friend's hand, but succeeded finally in taking a grasp of the board's edge. Quickly I slid down the remainder of the rope and clung to it with one hand while adding my support to the first boy.

There was now at least a chain of connection between Holmes and safety, formed of the two boys, myself and the rope, but the water was still churning and swirling violently and our fragile connections might be broken in a second by a particularly strong movement of the water.

'Lestrade!' I roared, for I knew that he was above me, peering horror-struck into the cellar. 'Lower the other rope!'

It seemed an age that I clung there, watching the boys and Holmes form a sort of circulation about the rope as a centre, before another rope fell past me. Quickly I seized it and bent it on to the one which I was holding, throwing the free end out towards Holmes.

My first throw fell away, diverted by the currents, as did my second, but at a third attempt I succeeded in landing the rope across the timber to which my friend clung. He snatched it immediately and secured it to his float, then began to haul himself towards me, motioning the two Irregulars to go ahead of him.

Soon all three were gathered beside me. Holmes was as pale as marble and gasping with exhaustion after his long exertions in the heaving waters, but he was evidently not injured.

'Holmes,' I said, 'climb up over me.'

'Nonsense, Watson!' he replied. 'These brave lads must go first.'

One after another the two urchins scrambled out of the water and over me, swarming upwards into the daylight. Only when they were safely on the pavement above did Holmes turn his mind to his own situation.

'I think,' he remarked, as coolly as though we were back in Baker Street, 'that we may require a little assistance. Perhaps Lestrade's merry men will help you and me to the top.'

So we ascended by the power of half a dozen pairs of brawny policemen's arms, to collapse at last, soaked, stinking and completely exhausted, upon the muddy cobbles of Deptford.

Twenty-One

Sherlock Holmes Fails

What Mrs Hudson might have thought if she had seen her two lodgers as we emerged from that fearful cellar, I cannot imagine. In the event she was spared a little of the impact, for Lestrade took us to Deptford Police Station, together with the two gallant Irregulars, where we had some opportunity to dry ourselves, remove some of the filth from our persons and take advantage of the Station's slop-chest for poor prisoners.

So it was that, some two hours after our escape from the rising waters, we were seated in the Station's staff room, supplied with enamel mugs of strong sweet tea and generous portions of bread and cheese, all of us clad in as random an assortment of clothing as I have ever seen.

Holmes' great height might have made him impossible to clothe from any but a police selection. As it was, only cast-off items of uniform had served the purpose, and he sat in a Constable's trousers and the braided former tunic of an Inspector, while I rejoiced in a seaman's canvas trousers that had seen better days and a thick woollen guernsey evidently knitted for someone a great deal larger than me.

The two Irregulars were delighted, not only at a free meal, but also at the opportunity to acquire some clean and whole clothing, one sporting a military bandsman's jacket in faded scarlet with decorative epaulets over a pair of cut-down policeman's trousers and elastic-sided boots, while his companion appeared in a carter's smock from beneath which poked a pair of battered sea boots.

Despite our washing and changing clothes there still hung about us all a distinct odour deriving from the slime and filthy water in the cellar and, grateful as I was for Lestrade's hospitality, I earnestly desired to take a long and thorough bath.

When Holmes and I had finished eating I noted that the colour had returned to his wan features. Turning to the Irregulars he thanked them in warm and sincere words for their selfless intervention. They both blushed to the roots of their scanty hair.

'Twern't nothing, Mr Holmes,' muttered one, from behind a doorstep of bread and cheese. 'Somethin' had to be done and you and the Doctor saw us out of that poisonin' business.'

I was touched by the way in which he spoke of himself and his comrade as a unit. Holmes searched in the unfamiliar pockets of his garments and produced a sovereign, sliding it across the table to the lads.

'That,' he said, 'will provide you and all your comrades with the means of holding a feast to honour the Irregulars for finding the organ-grinder, and yourselves in particular for your courage and intelligence.'

He turned to Lestrade. 'You know,' he said, 'that I do not court publicity, but I hope that you will find it possible to get these lads recognition from one of the societies that reward courage.'

'I can put their names forward, Mr Holmes,' began the Scotland Yard man, 'but I don't know as—'

Holmes interrupted him. 'If you are going to say that such societies may baulk at honouring two homeless street boys, then I would point out that our young friends have a hard existence before them. Anything that redounds to their credit should be properly recorded, so that it may be recalled for their benefit in the future.'

He stood up. 'Come, Watson,' he said. 'I feel we should not only shake the dust of Deptford from our feet, but also remove the traces of its geology, geography and wildlife from other areas of our persons.'

*   *   *

We were fortunate in our return to our lodgings inasmuch as Mrs Hudson did not witness our arrival. Nevertheless, even after we had washed again and changed into our own clothes, she sniffed the air suspiciously when Holmes summoned her to our sitting room.

Much of the remainder of the day was lost in a haze of steam and the perfume of soap, as our landlady's small household mobilized themselves to maintain a seemingly endless supply of hot-water cans to the baths in which Holmes and I sat steeping and scrubbing by turns, though even at our long-delayed dinner I was not sure that the traces of that miasmic cellar did not still hang about us.

When I came to the breakfast table next morning, it was to find that Holmes had already wired the hospital and been informed that Petrosino was still unconscious but had no life-threatening injury. A second wire arrived as we ate, this time from Lestrade. Holmes' features darkened as he read it and he tossed it across to me.

'Look!' he said. 'On my suggestion, Lestrade and the Surrey Police raided Corese's villa early this morning, for I feared that, believing Petrosino to be my agent, Corese would flee. That is exactly what has occurred. The house is empty and the bird has flown!'

I scanned the telegram. 'Where does this leave your enquiry?' I asked.

'Where it has been for seven years,' he said, bitterly. 'With Tosca dead and Corese gone, how is it possible to make headway?'

'Surely,' I argued, 'you have always said that Tosca and Corese were the planners of the theft of the Cameos, but that you wanted the actual killers of Father Grant. Since Corese seems always to have operated through henchmen already living in London, the killers are most likely still here and can be found, can they not?'

He snorted. 'Watson,' he said, wearily, 'neither you nor I nor anyone else knows how many persons of Italian or Sicilian ancestry or birth are presently living in and about

London. Even if a list existed that identified and located every one of them, how could I proceed? The killers are members of an association that takes deadly oaths and punishes treachery by torture and death. Even if we were to question the right men, they would assuredly lie, they would very probably produce unshakeable alibis and they would be supported in every way not only by their sworn fellow-criminals but by the wide population of fellow-nationals which they have terrorized into compliance. There is a case against them which would take them to the gallows if they can be identified. That identification might have come from Tosca or from Corese, but hardly from anyone else.'

He poured himself another cup of coffee, still with the same expression of frustration on his face. I was loath to see him acknowledge defeat after the astonishing efforts he had made, and tried again.

'It sounds impossible if you put it like that,' I agreed, 'but it cannot be so difficult in fact. The vast majority of Italian immigrants in London are hard-working and law-abiding people who can be ignored. Many of those who are not must be known to Scotland Yard, as must be the places where they foregather. Surely it would be possible to limit the number of suspects to a reasonable quantity and determine the actual perpetrators?'

I was delighted to see a slight smile pass across my friend's gloomy face. 'Upon my word, Watson!' he exclaimed. 'I had not realized how much of my methods you have absorbed! It might, as you suggest, be possible to achieve a result in that manner, but it might take a very long time and might, at the end, be frustrated by the very factors that I have mentioned – the sworn obligations of the perpetrators to lie, for themselves and for each other, and the support they will receive from seemingly innocent witnesses. No, Watson, I fear that the affair of the Vatican Cameos must be laid to rest among my failures and will never provide you with a source for one of your little narratives.'

We finished our meal in silence, both of us, no doubt,

dwelling internally on the great efforts which had led Holmes nowhere. We were not to know that a fresh aspect of the affair was, at that very moment, about to claim our attention.

Mrs Hudson arrived to clear our table, bringing the news that a 'clerical gentleman' was waiting below.

'Is it,' asked Holmes, 'that Irish poltroon who was here a couple of days ago?'

She shook her head. 'No, Mr Holmes. It is a much smaller man and of the Roman persuasion, I believe.'

'Show him up,' ordered Holmes, wearily. 'Who knows if he will not provide a little distraction from my failures.'

When our landlady had left he observed, 'It is almost a pity that it is not Cravat. After yesterday I believe I should be entirely justified in booting that mischievous idiot down our stairs.'

We were joined, moments later, by a short, plump man in the costume of a Roman priest. He wore wire-rimmed spectacles on his round and solemn face and his black clothing seemed to have seen hard wear. In one hand he clutched a worn briefcase and in the other a large umbrella. He peered about our sitting room myopically.

'Which of you gentlemen,' he enquired, 'is Mr Sherlock Holmes, the consulting detective?'

Holmes stood. 'I am he,' he said, 'and this is my friend and colleague, Dr Watson. Pray take the basket chair. I think you will find it the more comfortable.'

The priest accepted Holmes' advice and arranged himself in the basket chair, carefully setting his briefcase on the floor beside his rather large feet and propping his umbrella against the chair before adjusting his spectacles and looking round at us again.

'I am Father Brennan,' he began, 'and I have come to consult you, Mr Holmes, about a matter of great importance. It is only fair to you that I confess at the outset that I have no funds wherewith I might meet your fees, sir.'

He paused and peered anxiously at Holmes, as though expecting my friend to reject him.

Holmes waved a hand airily. 'My fees,' he said, 'never vary, save when I decide to remit them entirely. Such decisions are largely based upon the intrinsic interest of the case. Let me set your mind at rest quickly, Father Brennan. I am already instructed in an aspect of the matter which concerns you and have every hope that I shall be able to render a realistic note of my fees to my client in due course, so it causes me no hardship to listen to what you have to say.'

I had thought, illogically, that the appearance of a Roman priest in our sitting room indicated another aspect of the Vatican Cameos case and Holmes' remarks puzzled me. Only minutes before he had been declaring his enquiry a failure that must be laid away unsolved. How then did he hope to render an account to his client? Before I could resolve my queries the little priest spoke again.

'You are very kind, Mr Holmes, and you have taken a great weight off my mind. Now, perhaps, you will permit me to tell you what it is that worries me?'

'I know already what it is that worries you, Father Brennan,' said Holmes. 'What I do not know is which particular aspect of the case of Angelo Pisciotto concerns you?'

Father Brennan's face betrayed his astonishment and he fumbled at his glasses. 'Now, how did you come to know that, Mr Holmes?'

Twenty-Two

A Question of Faith

Holmes chuckled.

'It is my profession to know things which I have not been told, Father, and it was not difficult to divine your concern.'

'Might I ask what revealed my errand?' asked the priest.

'Certainly,' said Holmes, always cheered when strangers recognized his extraordinary skills. 'Firstly, I have been for a little while exercising my mind on the affair of the Vatican Cameos—'

'But they were stolen years ago,' interrupted our visitor, then checked himself. 'But of course, Cardinal Tosca was His Holiness' representative in Britain at the time. Do I understand you to mean that there is a connection between the death of Cardinal Tosca and the theft of the Cameos?'

'You are very astute,' said Holmes. 'At present I do not know if there is a connection. It is merely a possibility. If I may continue, my interest in the Vatican Cameos has led me to take some interest in the murder of the Cardinal and the arrest of Angelo Pisciotto.'

'But that would not reveal my interest,' said Father Brennan.

Holmes smiled. 'No, indeed, but your dress, while it clearly proclaims you to be a priest of the Roman Church, shows evidence of long wear and careful repair, as does your briefcase and your umbrella. You are not, therefore, a priest in a wealthy parish, so I took you to be one who ministers to the lower classes. The crucifix which you wear is unostentatious, but of craftsmanlike Italian workmanship.

138

Now, it might be a souvenir acquired by you or a colleague on a visit to Rome, but it might equally be an indication that you work among the Italian community. Finally, there is the question of your footwear.'

The little priest cast a rueful glance down at his somewhat large and rather shabby shoes.

'Like your clothing,' continued Holmes, 'your shoes betray long wear and careful repairs, but they also tell me something else, that you have walked here this morning from Pentonville, a surmise confirmed by your umbrella.'

'Pentonville! My umbrella!' exclaimed our guest. 'Really, Mr Holmes, this is most ingenious, but I fail to see how my shoes and my umbrella reveal a journey from Pentonville!'

Holmes smiled again. 'Your sturdy umbrella though damp is not wet. There was a brief shower of rain a little while ago and you were evidently out of doors at the time. That might have been anywhere in London, but you have been in the Pentonville Road, where the works connected with the relaying of a gas main have turned up quantities of a peculiar bluish-green clay which soils the pavement close to the prison gate. There are traces of it drying in the welt of your right shoe. It must have been a matter of some urgency which brought you directly to me from Pentonville, on foot on an inclement morning. I deduced that no one in Pentonville would be of more urgent concern to a priest of your faith at the present time than young Angelo Pisciotto.'

His exposition completed, Holmes sat back and observed Father Brennan's face, across which a range of expressions of astonishment were chasing each other.

'Upon my word, Mr Holmes!' he exclaimed at last. 'I had been told how very intelligent you are, but my experience has made me sadly aware that the possession of intelligence and the ability to apply it effectively are often separate. Never, however, have I witnessed such a display of accurate observation translated so rapidly into logical deduction. I hope that it augurs well for my decision to throw myself upon your charity.'

Honest acclaim always cheered my friend and he gave Father Brennan a warm smile. 'It is refreshing,' he joked, 'to meet someone who understands how I achieve my results. Most of Scotland Yard believes that I have some strange capacity for serendipitous guesses and many members of your profession seem to believe that I apply witchcraft.'

Our visitor smiled for the first time. 'The human brain is, perhaps, the greatest of God's creations, Mr Holmes. I am moved and encouraged to see the Master's work so well applied. May I tell you about the lad Pisciotto?'

'You must answer me a few questions first, Father Brennan,' said Holmes. 'I take it you have confessed the boy?'

'I have indeed.'

'And you will, of course, vouchsafe to me nothing that passed between you in his confession?'

'No, Mr Holmes, I will not.'

Holmes nodded thoughtfully. 'But you believe him innocent, else you would not be here.'

'I do.'

'Can I take it that you have information which is not embargoed by your professional confidentiality, Father?'

'I have talked to the boy at length, Mr Holmes, outside the sacrament of confession, and he is aware of my intention to seek your aid.'

'Very good,' said Holmes. 'Why do you think him innocent?'

Father Brennan produced a large handkerchief from a pocket, took off his spectacles and polished them earnestly before replying.

'If I were foolish,' he said, after replacing his glasses, 'I would seek to tell you that I had constructed from Angelo's information a case to meet the awful accusation that lies against him, but I hope I am not so stupid. In the first place my belief is founded upon faith.'

'Faith,' observed Holmes, drily, 'may move mountains, but Scotland Yard and the Central Criminal Court are not mountains. They are the very real and cumbersome obstruction which must be surmounted or bypassed by anyone who seeks to establish young Pisciotto's innocence.'

'Nevertheless, Mr Holmes, I would ask you to take that into account. It is a good many years since I put on the cloth and I have worked, as you rightly deduced, in poor parishes, and sometimes in rich ones. I have heard a good many stories, in and out of the confessional, Mr Holmes, and I hope that if I do not have your keen intelligence, I have at the very least learned to tell truth from falsehood.'

'Certainly it is a point to be considered, Father,' said Holmes, 'but we must also address ourselves to the facts of the matter.'

'If I might trespass once more, Mr Holmes,' said the little cleric, 'would you tell me if you believe young Pisciotto to be guilty?'

Holmes frowned. 'I do not know,' he admitted. 'At present I believe that there are considerable gaps in the case which Scotland Yard presents. I hope that you will assist me in widening them. Tell me about the boy.'

Father Brennan fumbled with his glasses again and looked at the floor, as though mentally rehearsing his presentation.

'Angelo Pisciotto is about eighteen – he is not sure of his birthday. He is a native of a little village in the hills of Sicily and a member of a family that is too large to support itself. For that reason he left home at thirteen and made his way to the coast, where he lived by doing casual work on the docks when he could get it and begging when he could not. One day he was offered work on a freighter, so he took to the sea. That, in turn, brought him to London about two years ago. The sight of our great capital had the same effect it has always had on wandering youths – it gave him the urge to stay here and see more of its wonders. In London he supported himself as he had in Sicily, by taking what work he could find or by begging. He has a quick ear for language and soon learned to speak a rough but serviceable English. Until his arrest he was working as an odd-job boy and messenger for the Benettis, who own the organ-hire business in Lantern Street.'

Holmes directed a significant glance at me, then asked, 'Has he any family in Britain?'

'He tells me not,' said the priest.

Holmes nodded. 'Inspector Lestrade tells me that the lad has admitted being in the vicinity of the Cardinal's hotel on the morning of the crime. Is that true, Father?'

Our visitor looked worried. 'It is. He has admitted as much to me, but he says that he went away without ever seeing His Eminence.'

'Why was that?' demanded Holmes. 'What was his business at the hotel?'

Father Brennan thought for a moment, then spoke slowly and carefully. 'He was carrying a message for the Cardinal.'

'From whom?' pressed my friend.

'That, Mr Holmes, I am not at liberty to say.'

'Very well,' said Holmes. 'You will forgive me if I assume that you know the name of the person whose message the boy carried. So, I think, do I, if he is telling the truth. You say that he failed to carry out his errand. Where did he go next?'

'He was concerned at his failure to do as he had been instructed. He wandered about for a little while, then visited the home of a young lady of his acquaintance. He remained there for most of the day.'

'Are there witnesses who can swear to his presence?' asked Holmes. 'Other than, of course, the young lady herself, who might be thought to have a personal interest in establishing his innocence?'

'That might be so,' agreed the priest, 'but her mother and sisters were present. Even her father saw him there later. It was the father's homecoming that caused young Angelo to leave.'

Holmes raised an eyebrow. 'The father does not approve of the relationship?'

Father Brennan shook his head vigorously. 'He does not, Mr Holmes. He has his own business and he sees Angelo as a penniless boy with no future. That was before the charge of murdering the Cardinal. Now he forbids his family to mention the boy.'

'So he will forbid his family to give evidence for Pisciotto?' asked Holmes.

Father Brennan nodded. Holmes passed an open hand down his long face, as though to wipe away the spasm of irritation that had crossed it.

'Was it then that he went to Mrs Ruggiero's boarding house?'

The priest nodded again. 'He did. He was afraid to go to his usual lodgings and he had stayed at Ruggiero's before.'

'And he entirely denies the murder of Cardinal Tosca? Or any part in it?'

'He does,' said the little cleric, stoutly. 'And I have told you that I believe him.'

Holmes steepled the long fingers of both hands before his face and remained silent for a long time.

'So,' he said at last, 'we have a young man who is identified by the hotel staff as being in the vicinity of the crime shortly before and who admits that he was so present but denies any involvement. He will not favour us with any explanation of his presence, nor of the reasons why he left without delivering his message. We have witnesses who saw him later but who will not speak, and we have your colleague, Father Cioffi, who I understand is quite certain that Angelo Pisciotto is the youth who presented a letter of introduction to him and who was the last person to visit the Cardinal before he was found dead. The case against him is circumstantial, but quite sufficient for him to be committed for trial and convicted.'

'You make it sound very black,' said Father Brennan, glumly. 'Is there nothing that can be done to help the lad?'

'It is not so black as if there had been witnesses to the murder or physical evidence that connected Pisciotto to the crime, or even any thread of reason that linked Scotland Yard's theory of events with Pisciotto's account. As to what may be done, Father, at present we must ask you to return with us to Pentonville. Watson, be a good fellow and ring for our boots. The good Father's capacious umbrella will see all three of us as far as the cab rank by Tussaud's without harm, I think.'

Twenty-Three

An Innocent Youth?

A ngelo Pisciotto sat at a plain deal table in a cell, his hands clasped about an enamel mug of tea and an impassive warder standing behind him. Being as yet unconvicted the boy was wearing his own clothing, a worn moleskin jacket with a bright neckerchief over a grubby yellow shirt.

The most immediate impression he made, even in his old clothes, was of his striking good looks. He was lithely built and had even features lit by the warm colour of his skin and by large, profoundly black eyes under the long lashes which are a feature of many Mediterranean peoples. A head of thick, black curls tumbled unkempt over his neckerchief. I recall thinking, with dismay, that the boy carried the kind of masculine good looks which, once seen, are seldom forgotten.

We seated ourselves around the battered table and Father Brennan introduced us. Holmes took out his case and offered Pisciotto a cigarette, but the youth waved it away politely.

'I thank you, Mr Holmes,' he said, 'for being so troubled as to come and see me, but I do not know what you can do that will get me out of this trouble.'

Holmes smiled, affably. 'Nor do I know, Angelo, but I believe that there are things which may be done and which may cast a different light on your position, if you will answer a few questions for me.'

The youth looked uneasily at Father Brennan. 'I will answer you all that I can,' he said, 'but Father Brennan knows that there are things I cannot say.'

'As to that,' said Holmes, 'I was not going to ask you about the message that you carried from young Signor Benetti to the Cardinal.'

The boy's jaw dropped and I felt Father Brennan start beside me. 'You know about the message?' he exclaimed. 'Have you told him, Father?'

'No,' declared Holmes. 'Father Brennan has kept your confession to himself. Let us just say that I know about the message because I have certain methods. What I do not know is why you did not deliver it. Will you tell me that?'

Pisciotto clutched his tea mug and looked about at each of us. Twice his mouth worked as though he was about to speak, but each time he said nothing. Then he lowered his head and spoke very quietly.

'I did not take the message to the Cardinal because I thought it was a wrong message, a wicked message.'

'Then I shall not ask you what it was,' said Holmes. 'Father Brennan tells me that you have no relations in England. Is that true?'

The boy cast a furtive and guilty glance at the little priest. 'I have an uncle in Birmingham, my uncle Giuseppe. I did not tell the Father because I was ashamed. I did not want my family at home to hear of the trouble I am in.'

Holmes nodded. 'And what family do you have at home?'

'There is Mama and Papa and I have seven sisters.'

'No brothers?' said Holmes, and the young man shook his head.

'So, your father must provide for good marriages for all those sisters,' said Holmes, 'and you decided to leave home to make things easier, yes?'

Pisciotto nodded. 'That is so,' he agreed. 'If my sisters do not marry well then we shall always be poor. I did not want that.'

'Tell me,' said my friend, 'why, when you came to England, did you not go to your uncle Giuseppe in Birmingham? What does he do?'

'He has the – I do not know what you call them – the presses, that is it. He has presses that make things from tin. He

145

makes whistles and toys, but he does not make much money and I do not really know him. He is my father's brother, but at home my uncles lived a long way away. We did not see them very often.'

'Does he have any children?'

'No, no. Uncle Giuseppe is not married. My other uncles at home, they have children, but I do not know who they all are. Like I said, they lived a long way away.'

'Do you know your uncle's address in Birmingham?'

'Yes, I do. My father gave it when I sailed to England.'

He recited an address in Birmingham, which Holmes jotted down in his pocketbook.

'When you left the hotel,' Holmes said, 'you have told Father Brennan that you wandered about for a while. Where was that and why was that?'

'I did not know what to do. I started to walk back to Deptford, but I was afraid, and sometimes I just stopped and sat by the road, trying to think about what I should do.'

'Of what were you afraid?'

'I had not done as Signor Benetti wanted. I was afraid I would be punished.'

'Or perhaps,' said Holmes, mildly, 'you had killed Cardinal Tosca and did not know where to go.'

The youth burst into a rapid stream of Italian, then switched to furious English. 'I did not! I did not! I was afraid of being punished – of being punished very bad. I did not kill the Cardinal! I would not do such a thing! If I am hung I shall die innocent and I can still go to Heaven, but if I killed the Cardinal I would be in Hell for ever!'

He had half-risen from his chair and the silent warder stepped forward and firmly pressed him back into his seat. He sat, shaking his head, and tears glistened on his cheeks.

'Very well,' said Holmes. 'Eventually you went to the home of a young lady, yes?'

'Yes, I did. She and her mother have always been very kind to me and I did not think where else I could go.'

'But you did not stay there?'

'I could not stay there. My – her father came home and he saw me there and he told me to go. He struck me and told me out of the house.'

'So you went to Mrs Ruggiero?'

'Yes, and I was still there when the police came for me. I had not done anything wrong and I did not run away from them. You ask them. I went along with them and I am in a prison and they want to hang me!'

'The clothes that you are wearing,' said Holmes, 'are they the same clothes that you wore when you went to deliver Benetti's message to the Cardinal?'

The boy looked confused. 'Yes. They are. I have not been able to change since that day.'

'Stand up!' commanded Holmes, with a nod to the warder. 'Open your jacket and hold it open!'

With a puzzled expression the boy did as Holmes required. My friend slid his lens from his coat pocket and leaned across the table to examine the front of the youth's shirt.

'Now button your jacket!' he ordered, when his examination was complete.

Again the lad followed Holmes' instruction, and again Sherlock Holmes ran his lens carefully all over the front of the jacket, before resuming his seat.

'Sit down, Angelo,' he said, 'and place your hands on the table, face up.'

Once again the lens was deployed in a minute examination of the fronts and backs of the youth's hands.

Holmes sat and stared thoughtfully at the boy for a full three minutes. Then he said, 'I have only a few more questions, Angelo. Firstly, you say that you carried messages for the Benettis. Did you know both of them – the older and the younger?'

'I know only old Signor Benetti who has his office at the warehouse. I took messages for young Signor Benetti, but I never saw him. I did not want to see him. People said he could be very angry and that he had terrible things done to people who made him angry.'

147

'I see,' said Holmes. 'Now, does the name Don Vittorio Corese mean anything to you?'

'Yes, Mr Holmes. Don Vito is from home, from Sicily. His family are very important. My father had his land from them. They own all the land for miles.'

'Did you ever see Don Vito?'

Angelo shook his head. 'No, no. He was gone to America years ago. I never saw him.'

'Very well,' said Holmes, standing up. 'If you have told me the truth, Angelo, I believe that I can help you out of your trouble. Good day to you.'

Outside the prison's gate the three of us huddled under Father Brennan's umbrella waiting for a cab.

'What do you make of the boy, Watson?' asked Holmes.

'I believe that he was trying to tell us the truth as he understands it,' I said.

'I agree,' said Holmes. 'His lie about his uncle was a simple and pointless evasion, which he admitted for himself. I wish I knew the content of Corese's message to the Cardinal.'

'I wish,' said Father Brennan, 'that I could reveal it to you, but you know my difficulty. I cannot, in conscience, give you any inkling of it.'

'I have an inkling of it, Father,' said Holmes. 'It is precise detail that I require and that, I suspect, is known only to Angelo and Corese.'

'Why do you call him Corese?' asked the priest.

'It is a long story, Father, and one that I will recite for you if you care to accompany us to Baker Street. I must send some urgent wires, but once that has been done I will try to put you in possession of the facts. My first duty, however, is to try and prevent Lestrade and his colleagues from hanging a valuable witness.'

Twenty-Four

Two Sides of a Coin

In the years that Holmes and I occupied 221b Baker Street, our landlady had a good many burdens to bear. Despite his avoidance of the fair sex, Sherlock Holmes was, in his own way, a nest-maker, who required an environment exactly suited to his needs and wishes. So it was that Mrs Hudson had to put up with his smelly table full of chemical experiments, his writing desk with its bulging pigeonholes, his all-night thinking sessions that choked the room with tobacco smoke, his disposal of his cigars in the coal scuttle, his tobacco in a Persian slipper and his unanswered correspondence nailed to the mantel with a knife, not to mention his occasional indoor pistol practice. In addition there were the irregular hours which he kept, making it impossible for her to plan the exact time of a meal. When it came to breakfast I was as great an offender as Holmes.

The exertions and dramas of the past few days, including our soaked and desperate efforts in and around that vile cellar, not to mention a severe clout from Cravat's henchmen, had begun to tell on me and, believing that Holmes would have no urgent need for me, I lay late in bed on the next morning. When eventually I arose it was to find that my friend was at the table before me, fully dressed and having largely completed his breakfast.

'You are about early,' I observed, as I poured myself a cup of coffee.

'Needs must,' he replied. 'Angelo Pisciotto will certainly be hanged unless I intervene successfully.'

'But I thought you believed the case against him to be full of holes?'

'So it is, Watson. So it is. But it does not take much to persuade a jury, particularly in a case where an important visitor to London has been murdered by an immigrant boy out of the Deptford slums. If there are Roman Catholics on the jury his position will be worse. They will be outraged by the murder of a statesman of their faith.'

'You paint a dim picture of British justice,' I remarked.

'Not without warrant,' he said. 'We persist in clinging to a system that encourages the police to make an arrest before they have taken any trouble to understand what has happened. The French system is infinitely preferable.'

I had been bred from childhood to believe in British justice, and could not let that pass.

'But that is inquisitorial!' I protested.

He smiled. 'By which, I imagine, you mean that Examining Justices in France obtain evidence with the rack, the thumb-screw and the boot! They do not. They ask questions in order to find out what has happened and then make a reasonable deduction as to the perpetrator. No, Watson, I cannot leave young Pisciotto to the mistakes and prejudices of an English jury.'

'Do you believe that you can save him?' I asked.

'It is a possibility,' he said, 'but one that requires certain urgent investigations. With that in mind I have drafted a number of telegrams. I shall be away much of the day, but I shall be back for dinner. Please see that any replies are kept for me.'

'Where are you going?'

'I must see Father Cioffi and I must visit the Pool of London, I suspect.'

He was evidently not going to invite me to accompany him, so I finished my meal while he skimmed through the morning papers, shortly after which he left.

His prediction was correct inasmuch as a number of telegrams were delivered throughout the day, all of which

I left unopened. To my surprise and, I suspect, that of Mrs Hudson, he was back at the stated time, apparently well pleased with his efforts for, after reading through the accumulated telegrams, he attacked his dinner with gusto.

We were filling our pipes after dinner when I tackled him about the Tosca case.

'Have your enquiries yielded any useful result?' I asked.

'Oh, indeed,' he said. 'For example, I have taken Father Cioffi to Pentonville and he has confirmed his identification of Angelo, as has one of the hotel's staff.'

'I really don't see how that helps,' I said.

'In addition,' said Holmes, ignoring my comment, 'Father Cioffi is not entirely sure that the clothes which Angelo now wears are those he wore at the hotel, but the hotel staff are certain.'

'And what does that mean?' I asked.

'Really, Watson! You saw me examine the boy's shirt and jacket. If they are the clothes which he wore at the hotel, then he certainly did not stab Cardinal Tosca while wearing them, nor did he climb down three floors of drainpipe in them.'

'How can you tell – about the drainpipe, I mean?'

'The climate of our city is notoriously wet, foggy and soot-laden, Watson. A drainpipe is made of cheap cast iron. Climbing down even a short length of London drainpipe, as you and I have proved on occasions, is likely to leave abrasions on the hands and clothing and engrained soot on the shirt or jacket. Angelo had none of those signs and no bloodstains on his clothing or beneath his fingernails.'

'Then you believe him innocent?'

'I have long harboured doubts about the matter,' he said. 'Now I am certain of his innocence.'

'But what of Father Cioffi's evidence?'

'Father Cioffi is telling the truth as he understands it.'

'But his story does not agree with the boy's version of events.'

'Come now, Watson. Angelo Pisciotto does not claim that Cardinal Tosca was not stabbed in his sitting room at the hotel by an assailant who most probably escaped by a drainpipe. He merely insists that he was not the murderer.'

'Yet Father Cioffi's evidence makes him almost certainly so!' I protested.

Holmes nodded, and taking a coin from his pocket he slid it across the table towards me.

'There,' he said, 'is a penny. On the one side is the profile of the Queen Empress, on the other a figure of Britannia in armour, guarding our shores. The images are totally different, are they not?'

'Of course,' I said.

'But they are, are they not, two sides of the same coin?'

'Of course,' I agreed again.

'We have the same thing here,' he said. 'Two different pictures which must be connected. Our task is to find the metal that lies between and makes both of them part of one rational series of events.'

'I do not see how that is possible,' I objected.

He laid two more coins on the table. I looked and saw that one was a farthing and the other a sovereign. Both had the Queen's portrait uppermost.

'Imagine, if you will,' he suggested, 'that this rather grubby farthing is brand new and highly polished. In a poor light, it might be mistaken for the sovereign.'

'Provided that both were displaying their obverse surfaces,' I agreed, reluctantly.

'Precisely, Watson. Despite the fact that the reverse of one bears an image of Saint George and the other of a robin, it is possible to make a genuine error about the obverse sides because they are so very similar.'

'I do not see,' I grumbled, 'how this relates to the murder of Cardinal Tosca.'

'In Tosca's case we have two different and mutually exclusive accounts of the actions of Angelo Pisciotto. You believe, and I agree with you, that the boy has told us the truth. I have seen Father Cioffi, and I believe that he is telling the truth. However, both of them cannot be correct. One of them must – albeit unconsciously – be wrong. We must find the point which has been wrongly perceived or remembered, so that we may discover what took place that morning and who was the guilty party.'

I had become entirely confused after his demonstrations with coins. 'I do not see how anyone can make sense of it,' I complained.

'When observation and recall are faulty,' said Holmes, 'the art of the reasoner comes into its own. We must, firstly, consider what might have happened within a reasonable framework.'

'Lestrade might be right,' I suggested. 'Perhaps the boy has fooled us and he is guilty.'

'It is a serious error, Watson,' said Holmes, sententiously, 'having reached a reasonable conclusion, to fling it away because it does not lead immediately to a solution of the problem.'

'There is no problem if young Pisciotto is lying!' I protested.

'Now there, Watson, you are wrong. If you follow that line it provides more problems than the present dilemma.'

He held out the fingers of his left hand and began to strike off his points with his right forefinger.

'Firstly,' he said, 'we know of no reason why the boy would have killed the Cardinal. Lestrade imagines an execution, the evidence suggests the Pompey Defence, but Pisciotto does not plead that excuse. Secondly, he carried no weapon with him. Thirdly, he drew attention to his real surname by presenting a letter of introduction to Father Cioffi. Fourthly, he succeeded in stabbing the Cardinal without attracting to his person or his clothing any trace of blood, and fifthly, he climbed three floors of drainpipe without injuring his hands or soiling his clothes.'

He sat back and watched me. I sat silent, recognizing that all his points were genuine and made nonsense of Lestrade's theory.

'Come, Watson,' he encouraged. 'Remember that, once

one has eliminated the impossible, whatever remains, however improbable, must be the truth.'

'But you say that it is impossible for the killer to have been young Angelo!' I complained.

He nodded. 'So you may eliminate that,' he said.

'But that,' I said, 'leaves Father Cioffi saying that someone who was, apparently, in every respect identical to Angelo Pisciotto, entered the Cardinal's sitting room and killed him, escaping by way of the bathroom drainpipe.'

Holmes nodded but remained silent.

'But that,' I said, 'is impossible in itself! Young Pisciotto would have had to have an identical twin, and we know that is not the case.'

Holmes nodded again.

'Then I give up!' I declared. 'I can only imagine that some monstrous coincidence has occurred whereby a youth who just happens to be an identical double of Angelo Pisciotto has committed the crime. If that is so, there is no way that the murderer can be found save by another monstrous coincidence. It all sounds like the plot of some dreadful melodrama.'

Holmes frowned. 'How often have you heard me remark, Watson, that coincidence is the willing handmaiden of a lazy mind? There is no coincidence here.'

'Then I say again that I give it up.'

Holmes smiled at me blandly and, picking up his pipe, began to fill it. 'You might,' he suggested, 'consider the Duke of York.'

Not another word would he speak that night about the death of Cardinal Tosca.

Twenty-Five

A Monstrous Coincidence?

L eaving the Great Western Railway terminus near New Street in Birmingham at mid-morning of the following day, I was still completely perplexed about the direction which Holmes' theories and enquiries were taking. Holmes' cryptic allusion to a Royal Duke had kept me awake long after I turned in, without making any connection that I could understand to the Tosca affair. In the morning, Holmes had chivvied me through a hurried breakfast, so that we might catch a Birmingham train, but without a word of explanation, and, while in transit, had chattered amicably and knowledgeably on almost any topic under the sun apart from the murder of the Cardinal.

Most of London smells of horses and oil, metal, wood, vegetables and cooking food, except the docksides and the manufacturing districts, where smells of brewery mash, chemicals and the river, tar and spices scent the air. Birmingham on a summer morning smelt much the same, apart from an underlying sulphurous odour, even in the centre of the city, deriving I suppose from the steam coal burnt all over the area.

A cab from New Street took us northward out of the city and soon we were bowling along streets where the hum of engines, the clangour of metal and the racket of many hammers could be heard all about. Workmen in greasy overalls, leather aprons or dustcoats emerged from one entrance of tall brick buildings and disappeared into another. It was about midday, and here and there a row of pale-faced factory

155

girls perched on a wall or railing outside their place of employment.

Eventually we were through the factory area and, turning aside from a main thoroughfare, entered a network of streets of terraced houses in red brick.

We had passed through several such streets when Holmes commanded our cabby to halt and wait for us, in the middle of a row which seemed indistinguishable from many we had traversed.

The house outside which we disembarked was a little larger than most of its neighbours and stood next to a wide entry. From the street we could see that the entry gave onto a cobbled yard with a workshop built across its far end. The front door opened directly to the pavement and Holmes stepped up to it and applied the knocker.

Very shortly the door was opened by a stocky man in early middle-age. He was dark-complexioned and black-eyed, but his hair and his thick moustache were both silver-grey.

'Mr Pisciotto?' enquired Holmes, raising his hat. 'Mr Giuseppe Pisciotto?'

'Yes, yes,' the man replied. 'I am Giuseppe Pisciotto, maker of fine stamped tinware and metal novelties. You are buyers, yes?' His accent was an extraordinary mixture of Italian and Birmingham.

Holmes ignored the question. 'We have travelled from London this morning,' he said, 'and I wonder if you would spare us a little of your time?'

Pisciotto smiled. 'Buyers from London?' he said, misleading himself as Holmes evidently intended. 'Usually you London people you wire ahead but I got no wire today. Still, never mind, come in, come in.'

We followed him in and he took us to a back parlour of the house, overlooking the yard and the workshop. There he insisted on pouring us wine from a straw-covered flask and offering us a plate of little sweet biscuits.

'Now,' he said at last, 'I never see you before, so I don't know what you know about me, but I got all the usual stuff, all the very cheap tin things – penny whistles, teetotums, diabolos. I got better things like guns that shoot matchsticks and carts and horses with wheels that go round. They going to cost a bit more, of course. Then I got my specials, I call them – things I do myself that no one else got. Let me show you my Beppo.'

Before Holmes could reply, our host had pulled from the drawer of a sideboard a device about twelve inches high. It seemed to be a ladder, its uprights made of coloured tin tubes slotted into a gaily painted tin stand and the two sides joined by metal rungs. I wondered at its purpose until Pisciotto reached into the drawer again and produced a small object which he balanced on the topmost rung of the ladder. I saw that it was a small coloured clown figure, slotted at the base so that it would rest on the ladder's rungs.

As Holmes and I watched, our host leaned forward and flicked the little clown gently with his forefinger. The figure lost its balance and swivelled over on its perch. As it dropped from the rung, when it seemed bound to fall to the table, a slot in the figure's head engaged with the second rung, so that it swung about that rung and then proceeded all the way down the little ladder, tumbling neatly from rung to rung until it came to rest seated on the lowest level.

'Bravo!' exclaimed Holmes. 'That is really a very amusing toy, Mr Pisciotto, and the control of gravity and rotation is cleverly employed, but I fear we have misled you. We are not here to buy your excellent manufactures.'

The Italian looked from one to another of us, with a puzzled expression.

'You are not buyers?' he said. 'But I thought you said you come from London?'

'Mr Pisciotto,' said Holmes, 'you have a nephew called Angelo, I believe?'

Our host's puzzled frown deepened. 'Yes, yes,' he said, slowly. 'But I not see him for years. My brother say his boy is in England somewhere, but I not see him.'

'I see,' said Holmes. 'Tell me, Mr Pisciotto, do you read the newspapers?'

The Italian's expression changed to one of embarrassment. 'No, no,' he said. 'I been here lot of years and I speak the good English so I can do my business, but I never read it so good. Maybe it is my eyes, but I don't read good.'

'So you have not,' persisted Holmes, 'seen a story about your nephew Angelo in the newspapers?'

'Angelo! In the newspapers?' Pisciotto shook his thick silver locks. 'What put little Angelo in the newspapers? What has he done?'

'He is in prison,' stated Holmes bluntly.

'In prison! Never! Not little Angelo. He was always a good boy to my brother and to his Mama. What for is he in the prison?'

'Murder,' said Holmes, even more bluntly.

Pisciotto half rose from his chair. 'Murder!' he exclaimed. 'Mama Mia! Angelo in prison for murder! This is very wrong. Angelo not kill anyone, he is a good, kind boy!' He paused and looked at Holmes. 'What are you, sir? A policeman?'

Holmes shook his head. 'No, no,' he said. 'I am someone who is trying to help Angelo because I believe that he is innocent.'

'Innocent! Of course he is innocent.' Pisciotto seized Holmes' hand in both of his. 'What can I do to help him? Does he need money? What does he need?'

'He does not need money, Mr Pisciotto, but he does need help. It is help that you cannot give, but your other nephew can.'

Pisciotto dropped Holmes' hand and leapt to the window. Flinging it open he shouted across the yard in urgent Italian, then returned to his seat and sat, shaking his head and looking from Holmes to me with a worried face.

I saw someone come out of the workshop and walk up the yard to the rear door of the house. A moment later the door of the room where we sat opened and a dark-haired youth entered and spoke to Pisciotto in Italian.

As the boy turned to take a chair I saw him better and was completely astonished. Although he was clothed in a very different fashion, wearing a cotton overall and a long leather apron, from head to toes the new arrival was a duplicate of Angelo Pisciotto in size, build, colouring and facial features. He sat and Pisciotto introduced him.

'Is this my nephew that you wanted to see?' he asked. 'He is Luigi, the son of my other brother. He has not long come from home. How can he help you?' Without waiting for an answer he turned to the boy. 'These gentlemen are from London,' he said. 'They have come about your cousin Angelo. They say that he is in prison – for murder – and they say that you can help, Luigi.'

The lad's dark skin paled and he licked his lips. 'What is it,' he said, in stilted English, 'that Angelo has done?'

'He has done nothing,' said Holmes, 'but he has been accused of murdering Cardinal Tosca and he is in prison about to be tried. I think that you can help him, Luigi.'

Young Pisciotto had gone even paler. 'How can I help Angelo? I have not seen him since we werc bambinos.'

'You can tell me,' said Holmes, 'how you called on Cardinal Tosca the morning after you came to London. You went to see him because you hoped that he would help you to find work and lodgings in London. You had a letter from a member of the Corese family in Sicily, introducing you and asking the Cardinal to assist you.'

Holmes paused, but the boy sat silent.

'You went to his hotel,' Holmes continued, 'and you presented your letter of introduction to Father Cioffi, the Cardinal's assistant. He showed you in to see His Eminence. While you were alone with the Cardinal, something happened.'

The boy still sat silent, his eyes like saucers and his hands clenched white against his grubby leather apron.

'Something happened,' repeated Holmes. 'At some point the Cardinal moved around his desk and took the chair next to you. Then he did or said something that startled and revolted you. I think, perhaps, he took hold of you. You were angry and sick at what was happening and you wanted to break away. Perhaps he held on to you, I don't know, but in your horror and fear you snatched a paperknife from the Cardinal's desk and struck him with it. He loosed his hold on you and toppled forward on to the carpet. For a second or two you were still filled with rage and disgust. You struck him two or three more times with the knife. Then you realized that you had killed him.'

Tears were streaming from the silent boy's eyes and he put up his hands to his face.

'When you knew that he was dead,' continued my friend, 'you sought a way out that would not take you back past the desk outside where Father Cioffi sat. You found the Cardinal's bathroom and went through its window and down into the street. Once out of the hotel you knew that you could not remain in London, so you fled to Birmingham, to your uncle here.'

Holmes stopped and looked at the youth. Luigi was crying like a child. 'You must have seen it!' he sobbed. 'You know it all! That is what I did, God help me! I murdered the great Cardinal. They will hang me and I will go to Hell!'

'I am not a priest,' said Holmes, 'but I do not believe any priest would tell you that you will go to Hell because you struck out in fear and anger and accidentally killed a man who had evil intentions against you – certainly not if you confess it. As to being hanged, there I can advise you with some authority. What I have told you and you have admitted would not be murder; at the most it would be manslaughter and for that you would not be hanged.'

The weeping youth raised his tear-stained face to Holmes and his eyes shone as though he had seen a light.

'On the other hand,' said Holmes, 'if Angelo were to be hanged as a result of your actions, I am not sure how a priest might see it.'

'Oh no!' the lad gasped. 'He will not hang, sir! I would never let my cousin Angelo hang for me!'

Twenty-Six

A Train of Deduction

There was always an element of the conjuror about Sherlock Holmes. Having reached some remarkable end to a train of deduction, he preferred not to reveal his thinking, but to present his audience – which, often, was only myself – with a spectacular result. He had never done so more successfully than in his finding Angelo Pisciotto's double.

As we settled into our seats on the train to London, I feared that he would divert the conversation from the Tosca affair without explaining his reasoning to me. As soon as the train was under way I tackled the point.

'Holmes,' I said. 'There have been many occasions when your reasoning out a solution to a problem has left me astounded, but never more so than at present. How did you do it?'

He smiled, thinly. 'So, I shall explain it all to you, after which you will say that it was "absurdly simple" – is that it, Watson?'

'Heavens, no,' I protested. 'I am really amazed by your discovery of Luigi Pisciotto and cannot imagine how you went about it.'

He laughed. 'Well, old friend, you would be right if you were to refer to the solution of this matter as "absurdly simple", for it was.'

'I do not see how it can have been,' I said.

He laughed again. 'So, you made nothing of my reference to the Duke of York last night?'

'Nothing at all,' I admitted. 'All I can recall about the Duke

161

of York is that he had ten thousand men, and he marched them up to the top of a hill and he marched them down again, and when they were up, they were up, and when they were down, they were down, and when they were only halfway up they were neither up nor down. What, however, that may have to do with the death of Cardinal Tosca I cannot imagine!'

He nodded, sympathetically. 'I was not,' he said, 'referring to that Duke of York. I had in mind the present Duke.'

'Prince George!' I exclaimed, seeing as little connection there as I had with the nursery-rhyme Duke.

'The same,' he said, taking his pipe from his coat pocket. 'Since the death of Prince Albert, the Heir Presumptive.'

'You are not,' I said, cautiously, 'implying a connection with the Royal family?'

He shook his head. 'No, no, Watson. I see that you have misled yourself completely.'

It was on the tip of my tongue to query his identification of the misleader, but I bit back the question. When he had filled and lighted his pipe he leaned forward.

'I was not jesting when I said that it was absurdly simple,' he said. 'Consider this – if Father Cioffi was recalling what actually happened, then Angelo Pisciotto was lying, and if Angelo Pisciotto was telling the truth, then Father Pisciotto was mistaken.'

'Of course,' I agreed.

'If, however,' he went on, 'Pisciotto was telling the truth and Father Cioffi was recalling what he believed had occurred, there would be only one reasonable solution – that a youth who strongly resembled young Angelo had called on the Cardinal.'

I nodded and he continued. 'Now, an extraordinary likeness may occasionally manifest in two people who are in no way related, but that is very unusual. The obvious place to find such a resemblance would be in a brother, and most particularly a twin brother.'

'But Father Brennan told us that Angelo has no brothers and the boy confirmed it.' I said. 'That is the point which concerned me last night. What I do not understand is how you arrived at the existence of Luigi Pisciotto and his resemblance to his cousin.'

'As so often, Watson, you put the cart before the horse. In one of our early arguments I put to you the possibility of deducing the existence of an ocean from a grain of sand, a proposition which you found required also a pinch of salt. Here I had arrived at the conclusion that there existed someone who bore an astonishing resemblance to Angelo. The problem was to identify that person.'

He puffed at his pipe for a moment. 'With no twin or sibling of any kind, I believed, nevertheless, that the most likely area in which to find such a likeness would be within the Pisciotto family. I was strengthened in that view by the use of the name Pisciotto by the killer. Now, I think you will agree that, outside twinship and brotherhood, the other relationships in which a close resemblance may appear are between parent and child or between cousins.'

'Cousins?' I said.

'Yes,' he said. 'Because they share common grandparentage. So I postulated the existence of a male cousin of Angelo's who would be about the same age, who bore a strong resemblance to Angelo and who was most probably called Luigi.'

'But we believed that Angelo had no family in England apart from his uncle in Birmingham. We heard him say so,' I protested.

'Not quite accurate, Watson. We heard him say so, and I am sure that he believed it, but it flew in the face of my deductions, so that I considered that he might be mistaken.'

'But how?' I said.

'Very simply. If he did not know that his cousin had arrived in England, that would indicate that the arrival had been very recent. I was encouraged in this belief by the letter of introduction, which would surely have been presented at the first opportunity after landing.'

'What did you do then?'

'I persuaded the Customs officials in the Pool of London

to assist me in reviewing the crew manifests of ships arriving from the Mediterranean shortly before the Cardinal's death, and in one such – the *City of Medina* – I found that a seaman named Luigi Pisciotto had taken his discharge in London on the day before Tosca died.' He smiled triumphantly.

'Wonderful!' I exclaimed, quite sincerely. 'But how could you be sure that he was not in London?'

'Italians,' he said, 'and in particular Sicilians, have a highly developed sense of honour. You saw how Luigi responded when he knew of his cousin's plight. Had he known of Angelo's arrest, he would have surrendered himself, but he had not, leading me to believe that he had fled from London. Now, he was recently arrived with no contacts in this country apart from the address of his uncle in Birmingham. The rest was easy, as you saw.'

'Wonderful!' I said again. 'Holmes, in the years of our association I have seen you produce a good many brilliant solutions to mysteries, but I have to say that there is an elegance to your deductions in this matter which leaves me astonished.'

He inclined his head. 'It is kind of you to say so, Watson, but I insist that the matter was a relatively simple one.'

A thought struck me. 'But where does the Duke of York fit into your theory?'

'Ah!' he exclaimed. 'I had overlooked His Grace. His function was merely that of confirming my view that a close resemblance often appears in cousins. You cannot be unaware that Prince George is almost a twin to his cousin, Nicholas of Russia.'

Despite my genuine admiration of his reasoning, I could have flung a seat cushion at his head when I considered the time I had spent on the previous night reciting that infernal nursery rhyme to myself and finding no sense in it.

'So!' I exclaimed, rather testily, I admit. 'It was, as I suggested, a monstrous coincidence.'

'It was no kind of coincidence, Watson. Coincidental events happen when there is no connection between them apart from their simultaneous occurrence. That is not the case here, where there are many connections, such as the connection between Tosca and Corese, for whom Angelo worked, or the family relationship between the two boys, or the fact that both of their families are tenants of the Coreses in Sicily. No, Watson, coincidence is a convenient excuse for the likes of Scotland Yarders, it will not do for me.'

Twenty-Seven

A Farewell Message

The days that followed were blissfully peaceful by comparison with our exertions in the Tosca affair. Holmes disappeared to the British Museum for whole days at a time, to pursue his arcane research into early British charters, while I caught up on my reading, strolled in the park and occasionally enjoyed a game of billiards.

Nothing more that connected with the case took place until the day when young Angelo was due to appear before the Justices for his case to be committed for trial. I had thought that Holmes might wish to be present, but I had reckoned without his hatred of newspaper publicity.

'There is no point, Watson, in my being there,' he said, when I raised the possibility at breakfast. 'I am fully aware of the hearing, but as I am neither a witness to nor a participant in the crime, I cannot see what evidence I might usefully give. On the other hand, if I attend as an observer, it will cause an unhealthy excitement in the penny-a-line reporters who cover the criminal courts and lead to unbounded speculation as to the reason for my presence. That would not please our friend Lestrade, whose face will be red enough in all conscience.'

'You don't mean to say that you are going to let him take the credit for solving the case again?' I protested.

'Why not, Watson, why not? He will be embarrassed by the undoubted fact that he arrested and charged the wrong lad. I can at least offer him the opportunity to shine as having put the matter right in the end.'

'You are altogether too generous,' I grumbled.

'It is not a question of generosity,' he said. 'I have had the intellectual satisfaction of seeing my theories work out in practice. That is all that I require. Lestrade, to maintain both the public's perception of him and that of his superiors, must go further than that, so I have let him do so.'

It was useless to argue with him once he had made up his mind, so I settled myself after breakfast with the morning newspapers and tried to keep my mind off the case. Nevertheless, I could not help an occasional glance at the clock on the mantel, to see if the committal hearing might yet be over.

It was almost time for luncheon when Mrs Hudson announced Father Brennan. He came in, breathless and beaming broadly. Once Holmes had seated him in the basket chair and I had supplied him with a brandy and soda, he began his story.

'The Prosecutor,' he said, 'was Mr Burnett. He's young, but sharp, and I have seen him send men to the gallows before. He outlined the case to the Justices, saying that it was an unexplained killing of an important visitor to these shores, a man held in respect by many who shared his faith and a man known to be the most senior advisor to the Holy Father. I thought he was laying it on with a trowel, as it were, but he went on in the same vein. He said that Father Cioffi would identify the killer beyond any shadow of a doubt and that, having heard the witness, Their Worships would have no choice but to commit the prisoner for trial as charged.'

He paused to sip his brandy and resettle his spectacles. 'Then he called Father Cioffi,' he went on. 'The Father was calm and collected in the witness box and told his story well, but I won't bore you with repeating it. When he had done, Mr Burnett said, in a very dramatic voice, "And that youth who presented the letter of introduction – do you see him in Court?" Well, of course, Father Cioffi pointed at Angelo in the dock and said, "That's him," and Burnett said, "Are you quite certain?" and Father Cioffi said, "Absolutely," and Burnett closed his evidence and sat down.'

He sipped again and continued. 'Then up pops Mr Thompson for Angelo. Now, he's younger than Burnett, but he does a lot of defences for poor prisoners. He says to Father Cioffi, "You are a man in Holy Orders, and you have sworn on the Bible that the man in the dock was the man who presented a letter of introduction to you and whom you admitted to the Cardinal's room. Are you sure of that?" "I am," says the Father. "Well now," says Thompson, "can you tell us what was the name on the letter of introduction? Who was it introducing to His Eminence?" "Luigi Pisciotto," says the Father, and Mr Thompson nods. "Luigi Pisciotto," he repeats. "And is that the name of the Defendant?" "No," says Father Cioffi. "I understand him to be called Angelo Pisciotto." Mr Thompson nods again, then he says, "Have you ever met a lad called Luigi Pisciotto except that morning?" "No," says the Father, looking a bit perplexed and who could blame him. "Well then," says Mr Thompson, "perhaps it's time I introduced you," and he calls out, "Bring in Luigi Pisciotto!"'

He paused again and his smile widened. 'Ah,' he said. 'You should have seen it, Mr Holmes, Doctor. It was better than a play. An usher brings in Luigi and stands him by the dock, right by his cousin, and Mr Thompson says, "This, Father, is Luigi Pisciotto. Now, can you identify the young man who came to the hotel on the morning Cardinal Tosca was killed?" And the Father holds his head down and at last he says, "No. I cannot be certain any longer." Then Thompson says, "No further cross-examination, Your Worships, but I'd like to call a witness," and he motions young Luigi into the witness box. He swears him and has him give his name and explain that he arrived from Sicily the day before the Cardinal was killed and that he had gone on that morning to present a letter of introduction to His Eminence in the hope of finding work and lodgings, and that Father Cioffi had admitted him to the Cardinal's sitting room. At that point the Chairman of the Bench intervened. He said, "Mr Thompson, this must go no further. He must be warned of his right to avoid self-incrimination. I do not think we need to hear more. Have you a submission?" So Mr Thompson submits that the Prosecutor has not made out a case for trial and the Bench agrees and they discharge Angelo with any costs he has paid or that have been paid for him against the police. And that was that. Burnett was sitting with a face like a sour pudding and Lestrade was behind him, looking gloomy, and all the reporters are about to leave for an early special edition, when Luigi walks across the Court and holds out his hands to Lestrade. The Inspector stares at him for a moment, then he formally arrests him and takes him out, telling the press boys that this is the real killer of the Cardinal, as if he'd always known it.'

'Ah yes,' murmured Holmes. 'The good Inspector always recovers his poise rapidly.'

'But I must ask you, Mr Holmes,' went on our guest, 'what do you think will become of Luigi now that he has admitted murdering the Cardinal?'

Holmes shook his head. 'It was not murder, Father. The circumstances which I postulated and which he described would make it killing in self-defence or, at the least, through provocation. Either would make it manslaughter. In the end, however, the decision as to the charge lies with Scotland Yard and the outcome may lie with a jury.'

'But you do not think he will hang?' pressed the priest.

'I think you had best ask Lestrade,' said Holmes, and the words had barely left his mouth when the door opened and Mrs Hudson appeared, followed by the Inspector himself.

'Ah! To name the Devil!' exclaimed Holmes, with a swift wink at Father Brennan. 'Come in Lestrade! We were just discussing your remarkable triumph this morning.'

The detective had at least the grace to look slightly discomfited as he seated himself. 'I have come, Mr Holmes,' he announced, 'to tell you what took place this morning, but I see that Father Brennan has beaten me to it.'

'So he has,' agreed Holmes, smilingly, 'but he has given full weight to your own part in the hearing.'

Lestrade frowned slightly. 'Mr Holmes, I know that we have had many differences of opinion over the years and that you have often had the better of me, but I hope I have never been a bad loser.'

'No, no, Lestrade. In all our differences you have been the first to acknowledge my little successes. If you can take any credit from Luigi Pisciotto's confession, you are welcome. We both serve the cause of justice.'

'You are very gracious, Mr Holmes, very gracious,' said Lestrade. 'You saved us from hanging an innocent boy,' and he shuddered slightly at the thought.

'We were discussing,' interposed Father Brennan, 'whether or not Luigi Pisciotto is at risk of the gallows, Inspector.'

'It's early days, Father, but I shouldn't think so. As soon as I got him back to Cannon Row, there was a solicitor already there, instructed on the boy's behalf by no less than the Cardinal Archbishop, and strong representations were made that his offence, if there was one, was manslaughter at the worst. We haven't made up our minds about a charge yet.'

Holmes arched an eyebrow. 'Does that mean that you may yet not bring any charge against him?'

'Between us here,' said Lestrade, 'that's a possibility. After all, if he were to plead to manslaughter, that'd be no problem to anybody, and in the circumstances he'd get as light a sentence as could be given, but this solicitor he's got seems to think that he's got a good defence to manslaughter as well. So, if he's charged there may well be a trial.'

'And that,' said Holmes, 'is what nobody really wants.'

'Well, it certainly wouldn't do anybody any good, Mr Holmes. Let's say it would only lead to a washing of dirty linen in public.'

Holmes nodded and Father Brennan said, 'Oh, I do hope there will be no charge made.'

'Well, Father,' said Lestrade, 'if you were Dr Watson here, you might lay a sovereign or two on that without much fear.'

The wide smile returned to the cleric's face and he bent to fumble in his briefcase.

'And what,' asked Holmes, 'will become of his cousin Angelo? He can hardly stay in London, at risk from members of the Rule of Nine, nor can he return to Sicily.'

Father Brennan straightened up, clutching a sheet of paper. 'I have managed,' he said, 'to find someone who will pay the lad's passage. He had hoped to reach America, but that is another place where he would not be safe, so he is bound for Australia. Now that he has been freed, there is nothing to stop him sailing tomorrow.'

He paused and looked around at all of us. 'I know,' he went on, 'that you think my silence over matters vouchsafed to me in Angelo's confession was not helpful, though I think you understood my situation. Well, Mr Holmes, I can tell you now that Angelo has freed me of my obligations and given me this.' He held out the paper to Holmes. 'It is the message that he carried from Benetti to the Cardinal, and you may see why he believed it to be a wicked message.'

Holmes took the paper and scanned it rapidly. A slow smile spread across his face. 'It is in Italian,' he said at last, 'and bears no address or greeting, but if my Italian serves, it says, "The goods are worth at least as much again. If that is agreed, I will give you the persons you need. They have served their purpose in any case, so they will be no loss to the Nine. They have got above themselves lately and taken to politics. If it matters to you they can be hanged. Their names are Giovanni Carella, Pietro Nicolo and Rosario Mancini."'

He looked up at us. 'If this is true, we have the killers of Father Grant,' he said.

'If they can be found,' I remarked.

'That first name,' said Lestrade, 'Giovanni Carella. I know him. We put him away for five years for stabbing someone in a brawl. When he came out I went to visit him. It's right that he took to politics. He's an anarchist. I called on him when he came out, by way of letting him know we were still watching him. He lives in Burgage Street, over a catsmeat shop. Those other two must be the fellows that share with him.'

'Then,' said Holmes, 'we have our prey and we know his lair – now we must set about trapping him.'

Twenty-Eight

Under the Red Banner

I was woken early the next day by Holmes pressing my shoulder. He was already fully dressed.

'Come, Watson,' he commanded. 'We must meet Lestrade before daybreak.'

We broke our fast hastily on coffee and toast, then wrapped ourselves warmly, for the summer morning was still cold, and set out to our rendezvous. At Holmes' suggestion I had my Adams .450 in my overcoat pocket, with a box of cartridges. Holmes too was armed.

'We know these are ruthless men,' he said, 'who have killed with a firearm when it was not necessary. We cannot tell how they may respond if we succeed in cornering them.'

Our cab retraced much of the route we had taken to rescue Petrosino, though more directly, for the streets were largely empty. Our hooves and wheels echoed in the sleeping streets and more loudly as we trotted beneath the great piers of Tower Bridge, where the reflected stars gleamed at us from the river on either side.

Soon we were in Deptford and disembarking at the corner of a riverside street. Lestrade was there before us, waiting with a posse of uniformed constables armed with both pistols and shotguns.

'Good morning, Mr Holmes, Doctor,' he greeted us. 'So far everything's going according to plan. That's the house, over there.' He walked to the corner and pointed to an old three-storey house backing on to the river, its ground floor displaying a peeling shopfront with dusty windows and a faded sign advertising catsmeat.

The plan had been made at Baker Street on the previous day and Holmes and the Inspector now rehearsed its points.

'What about the other occupants?' asked Holmes. 'Are they safe?'

Lestrade nodded. 'Father Brennan's done his bit,' he said. 'He volunteered to go in and wake them quietly and get them out. I've sent them all down to Deptford nick. A free breakfast and a couple of mugs of strong tea and they'll be happy as sandboys.'

'Has the landlady confirmed that Carella and his companions are in residence? It would be a pity to spend so much effort in flushing an empty covert.'

'Oh, yes. They're in there alright.'

'Do we know any more about the interior of the house?' Holmes said.

'Indeed we do,' said the police officer. 'Father Brennan has done me a little sketch.'

He drew a paper from inside his overcoat and displayed it to Holmes and me. 'You see,' he said. 'That door by the catsmeat shop only goes into the shop. There is a back door to the shop, but that's locked when the shop's not open. There's no front door into the house, you have to go into that entry on the left. That goes through to the backyard and the river bank, but there's a side door from the entry into the house.'

He turned the paper over to show two more sketches detailing the upper floors. 'When you go in, the shop's in front of you and the passage goes right to the bottom of the stairs. There's a kitchen and scullery behind the stairs on the ground floor. Up the stairs, there's two rooms, one opening through the other. The door to them is on your left. Those rooms have got windows,' and he pointed across to the house.

'Up the stairs again is the same pattern, two rooms, one opening from the other, and again two windows at the front, then beyond that is a narrow stair up to the attic, that's where

Carella and his pals have been staying. The stairs end right in front of the attic door, and the attic is divided into two.'

'Has the attic any windows?' enquired Holmes, scanning the front of the building earnestly.

Lestrade pointed again. 'Do you see them two small windows, right up under the eaves? Those are the attic windows.'

Holmes nodded. 'So, the house is now empty of all except Carella's gang, yes?'

'So far as I know, yes, Mr Holmes. That's unless they've got somebody up in the attic with them.'

'What back ways are there out of the house?' asked Holmes, turning back to Father Brennan's rough diagrams.

'There's a back door from the scullery and another by the foot of the stairs, Mr Holmes.'

'Do not these old riverside buildings have balconies at the back?' asked my friend.

'There's a rickety old wooden balcony across the first floor,' confirmed Lestrade, 'but it wouldn't take them anywhere. There's no steps from it. You can only get on and off it from the first-floor sitting room.'

'You have the River Police in place, as we agreed?' said Holmes.

'Yes, indeed. There are two launches lying out in the river. Luckily there's been thick mist on the water since we got here, so you can't see the boats from the land.'

'Excellent!' exclaimed Holmes. 'There is evidently a footway at the rear, between the house and the waterside. Are there any jetties nearby?'

'There's no jetty immediately behind the house,' said Lestrade, 'but there's one that juts out about three houses upriver. I've got one man at the back, keeping obbo from behind that jetty.'

'Well done, Lestrade,' said Sherlock Holmes. He pulled out his watch and opened it, then looked downriver, where the first signs of dawn were appearing in the sky. 'Hopefully our quarry are still sleeping. So long as the mist holds on the water they will not spy the police launches. I suggest that, once there is a little more light, we go in and hope to surprise them.'

'I cannot allow you to enter,' said Lestrade.

'Tush!' ejaculated Holmes. 'You cannot prevent me, Lestrade. Besides, Watson and I are a good deal more experienced at this kind of thing than your Constables. No, when the time is ripe – which will be very soon – we shall enter the house as silently as we may. Your officers can secure the ground floor, but I do not wish to be accompanied by the tramp of regulation boots as I climb that narrow stair to a door behind which three armed killers may or may not be asleep. Once Watson and I have breached the attic, your men may follow us.'

'I do not like it, Mr Holmes,' protested the little detective.

'I cannot say,' replied Holmes, 'that I view the prospect of that narrow attic stair with any great pleasure myself. Nevertheless, the job must be done and it will soon be light enough to do it.'

He took out his cigarette case and we stood smoking and watching the dark and silent house across the street. The daylight strengthened in the east and when our cigarettes were done, Holmes said, 'Come, Watson. Let us try conclusions with the Rule of Nine.'

He stepped briskly around the corner and strode towards the house with me a pace behind. As we approached I saw no light or sign of movement in any window. Holmes slipped quickly into the dark entry beside the catsmeat shop and from there into the hall of the house, where we waited for Lestrade's men to catch up. A half dozen Constables made a creditable job of traversing the street silently and slipped in behind us. The leading officer looked expectantly at Holmes for instructions.

'Stay here and remain absolutely still and quiet,' whispered Holmes, 'until Watson and I have got into the attic. Then we shall want you with us as fast as possible and noise will be no objection.'

'Shouldn't we be closer behind you than that?' whispered the officer.

'Perhaps,' said Holmes, 'but only if you can maintain absolute silence. When we go up, three of you take off your boots and follow us to the foot of the attic stair.'

He started up the first flight of stairs, moving silently himself, and I followed, nervous at every step of the old wooden stairs beneath our feet. Nevertheless, by treading close to the inner edge of the steps we managed to move with very little sound and were soon at the foot of the narrow stairway to the attic.

Holmes paused for the stockinged officers to catch us up, then stepped softly as a cat up the last few stairs. At the top he laid a hand gently on the door handle and tried it softly. It gave way to his hand and he smiled at me and pulled his pistol from his overcoat pocket. I drew my Adams and moved closer to my friend. As Holmes jerked open the door we sprang into the room almost simultaneously.

At such moments one is inevitably tensed to expect a violent outcome. We could not know whether we might be shot at or assaulted as we entered the attic. For this reason, the senses are wrought to their highest pitch and the reflexes at their fastest. So it was with Holmes and I, and so the feeling of anticlimax was the greater when we discovered the long, dim room to be empty.

The area which we had entered appeared to be their sitting room and smelt of coarse wine, spirits and garlic. It was furnished with threadbare rugs on its board floor and a selection of ancient and well-used chairs around a plain deal table whose top was smeared with wine and food stains and much scarred by tobacco burns.

Holmes glanced quickly about him then stepped purposefully to the rear door with his pistol still in hand. Again I followed so close that we entered almost as one.

The far room was darker and contained three single beds. For a second I thought that there were bodies in one or more of them, but as my eyes became accustomed to the thin light creeping through the dusty windowpanes I realized that what I saw was heaps of blankets where the beds' occupants had tumbled out and left them in disarray. Apart from the beds there was no furniture, but beside each cot stood an upturned orange crate, to serve, I imagined, as a bedside table.

'The birds have flown!' exclaimed a voice immediately behind me, startling me until I realized that our stockinged reinforcements had followed silently.

Holmes was pacing about the room, peering closely at the tops of the improvised bedside tables. He had just removed something from one of them and slipped it into his pocket when we heard the distant sound of a policeman's whistle from the rear of the premises.

Holmes stepped to the single rear window and flung it up. The whistle was still sounding, now louder, its bursts interrupted by cries of 'They're out! On the balcony!'

'It is Lestrade's lookout,' said Holmes. 'He has spotted them escaping.'

He leaned out of the window and craned to his left. Seconds later a bullet struck the outer wall near his head and he withdrew.

'Quickly!' he snapped. 'They are escaping across the balcony roof! We must get down and stop them!'

Helter-skelter we plunged down the stairs and tumbled out into the side entry. Lestrade and his men were already moving into the alley to reach the rear of the house in response to their colleague's message. Our three supporters were forced to stop and recover their boots, but the rest of us pressed through the entry, into the littered rear yard of the house and on to the riverside.

Behind the yard was a cobbled footway flanking the river. To our left we could see three figures scrambling down the supports of the rickety balcony of a house further along. It was evident that they had escaped from our trap through the first-floor rear window on to the balcony and made their way along the row from roof to roof across the balconies. Now they were intent on reaching a small jetty that protruded into the river close to where they were climbing down.

Suddenly a figure appeared, standing up behind a rainwater butt beyond them. It was the Constable that Lestrade had posted. 'Stop!' he shouted at the Italians. 'In the name of the law!'

He was answered by a shot, which took him in the shoulder and spun him round, to fall back behind the large barrel.

Holmes waved us all forward, and Lestrade and I, backed by the Inspector's men, charged along the waterside in an effort to prevent the fugitives reaching the jetty. A hail of fire from three pistols met us, but we carried on, crouching, weaving and attempting to return fire as we ran.

The distance was too great and their fusillade slowed us sufficiently for them to reach the far end of the little jetty, where they disappeared behind a stack of crates and barrels. Holmes raised a hand to stop our advance and we withdrew into the space between two houses.

'We've still got them, Mr Holmes,' declared Lestrade. 'They can't see the River Police yet for the mist, but they're penned in now, between us and the river boys.'

'Yes,' agreed Holmes, 'but they seem to have no lack of ammunition and to be prepared to sell themselves dear. If the launches try to take them from behind they will open fire, and if we try to rush the jetty they will take more than one of us before we reach them. There must be a way that will not risk any loss of life.'

'If I might offer a suggestion,' said a quiet voice from behind us, and we turned to see that Father Brennan had found his way to us between the buildings.

'What do you suggest?' asked Holmes.

The little priest fumbled with his owlish spectacles. 'It seems to me,' he said, 'that Mr Holmes is right. If any of you approach the jetty they will shoot.' He paused. 'On the other hand,' he said, 'they might not be so quick to shoot at someone who poses no threat to them.'

It was a moment before his meaning dawned on us. 'You

can't mean to go yourself!' said Lestrade. 'I won't allow it! If you were to get harmed the Commissioner would have my job off me!'

'You know, Father, that these are desperate men in a tight corner,' said Holmes. 'They have killed at least once. Why would they not kill you?'

'They are sons of my Church,' Father Brennan said quietly.

'In name only, Father!' said the Inspector. 'I know Carella. He's an anarchist – he has no religion. Mr Holmes is right, they shot Father Grant out of hand and they'll do the same to you. No, I can't allow it.'

'I don't think that they will so far forget their childhood faith as to shoot down an unarmed man in cold blood,' the priest said.

'They have done it once,' said Holmes, and drew something from his pocket. He displayed it on his open palm and I saw that it was the ornamental American watch-case which I had seen on Petrosino's waistcoat when we first met. 'What is more,' he said, 'I found this in their bedroom. They are evidently the persons responsible for the attempt on Petrosino's life.'

Father Brennan's expression did not change. 'It is my duty,' he said, 'and with all possible respect to you, Mr Holmes, and to you, Inspector, you will not prevent me.'

He looked away from us, towards the jetty, and his lips moved silently for a few seconds, then he crossed himself, braced his shoulders and marched off, swinging his umbrella like a walking stick.

We watched him in silence as he marched along the riverside, expecting shots at any moment. None came, and he continued until he stood on the ancient jetty. Only then was there a response to his action.

'Get away, priest!' a voice shouted from the refuge at the jetty's end. 'Go away or we will shoot!'

'I have come to talk to you,' replied the little priest.

'We do not want to talk to you!' cried the voice. 'Go away, or we will shoot!' and the command was underlined by a single shot, fired over the cleric's head. 'Get away now,' continued the voice. 'We have shot one of your kind. What matter will another make?'

'You have done the bidding of an evil man,' said Brennan. 'It does not mean that your sins cannot be forgiven.'

'No? But it still means that we will hang! We do not want your mumbo-jumbo, priest. We are not among your foolish followers any more. So, we did the work of Don Vito Corese, and what is he? You call him an evil man, but he is no more evil than any capitalist. He is a rich man who lives like a pig while he has others to sweat and steal and kill for him. So is the King of Italy and the President of the United States and the Queen of England and your Holy Father in Rome. One day we anarchists will hang them all, every one, and every priest too.'

This tirade ended in a spatter of shots, all of which missed the brave little priest, though many struck the planking around his feet.

He raised his hand and made the sign of the Cross. 'I shall pray for you,' he called, and turned slowly away. Still clutching his umbrella he trudged back along the jetty.

Holmes frowned. 'I had hoped,' he remarked, 'that we had a slender chance of ending this without bloodshed, but not now,' and he pointed.

Above the barricade of barrels and crates on the jetty a length of timber had appeared and from its end fluttered a scarlet neckcloth.

Hoarse cries of 'Bandiera rossa! Avanti popolo!' rang along the riverside.

'It appears that it has become a political war,' remarked Holmes.

'What are they shouting?' asked Lestrade.

'Anarchist slogans,' replied Holmes. 'The red banner! Forward the people! The usual humanist mottos for which the genuine believer will die but Carella's sort will kill.'

'I told you they're anarchists,' said Lestrade glumly. 'You heard what they said about Her Majesty.'

Twenty-Nine

Surprising Conclusions

Holmes had his head sunk in thought, his right hand wrapped about his chin. Suddenly he raised his head. 'This must end,' he announced, 'and swiftly.'

He looked at the mist, which was now beginning to disperse from the water's surface under the impetus of the climbing sun and a slight breeze from the west. Upriver towards Tower Bridge a tug hooted and another replied.

'Listen!' said Holmes. 'The river traffic is beginning to move as the mist clears. We must arrest Carella and his companions before boats start moving down this reach.'

'Easier said than done,' observed Lestrade.

Holmes wet a finger and held it to the breeze. 'Perhaps not,' he said. 'Watson, stay here with Lestrade. He may need your skill with a pistol. Lestrade, wait for my signal.'

'What will it be?' asked the bewildered detective.

'You will know it when you see it,' Holmes replied and, slipping like an eel through the cluster of Constables behind us, he was gone.

Lestrade and I simply looked at each other wordlessly. Accustomed as we both were to my friend's sudden, unrevealed decisions, neither of us could fathom his present plan.

The mist was now breaking up fast, and soon I became aware of dark shapes beyond the jetty on the river and realized that they must be the River Police launches. Not long after, a shot rang out from the jetty, calling a response from one of the launches, and soon there was a brisk exchange of gunfire between the boats and the men pinned down on the jetty.

'I wish,' said Lestrade, striking one fist into the other palm, 'that we could get up against them on this side. The river lads have got them fully occupied. We could take them unawares.'

'It won't do,' I said. 'There's not a trace of cover between here and the jetty. They'd just mow us down.'

We continued to watch and listen to the exchange between the Italians and the River Police. Soon I thought that I detected a difference in the pattern of gunfire.

'I do believe they're conserving their ammunition,' I said to Lestrade. 'They must be running low. Perhaps this is our opportunity.'

I looked along the riverside, considering whether it was yet possible to charge the jetty. Nothing had changed apart from the presence of an old man in the distance. Beyond the water butt where Lestrade's Constable lay wounded, the man was raking what seemed to be rags from the yard of a house and piling them on the cobbled footway by the river. As I watched, he paused, took a pipe from the pocket of his old dustcoat and lit it. Still holding the match he stooped and applied it to the mound of rags that he had created.

In seconds a thick column of smoke, in twisted skeins of white and black, rose from the fire and, snatched by the strengthening breeze, began to drift towards us along the river's bank.

'That's it!' I exclaimed. 'That's Holmes' signal, Lestrade!'

'Blimey!' he said. 'So it is! When that smoke reaches us we'll be able to sneak up on our friends while they're trying to keep the boats at bay.'

Soon the smoke cloud was all about us and Lestrade and I led the posse of Constables silently along the bank towards the jetty. Not a shot was fired in our direction and soon we were almost at the landward end of the jetty.

Suddenly Sherlock Holmes materialized out of the smoke. 'Well, Lestrade,' he remarked, 'they seem to be low on ammunition and now they are trapped between us and the launches. Shall we take them?'

Lestrade stepped on to the jetty and we followed. Peering through the fringe of the smoke we could see that Carella had rearranged his defences so as to protect his group from the fire from the launches. They were completely exposed to us and they seemed to have stopped shooting. Lestrade was about to move forward again when Holmes held him back.

'Wait!' he commanded. 'What are they doing?'

Two of our quarry were pressed close against their barricade of crates and barrels, each holding a pistol, but the third was doing something with an object at his feet. A match flared and the man straightened up.

'Avanti popolo! Bandiera rossa!' rang out again.

'Back!' cried Holmes and plunged off the jetty, dragging Lestrade and me with him on to the cobbles. The confused Constables followed their Inspector and when Holmes shouted 'Down!' they obeyed his command while he dragged Lestrade and me to the ground.

As I lay, winded and puzzled, on the shore, there was a huge roar from behind me and I saw a flash of brilliant orange reflected on the cobblestones near my head. A rain of debris, fragments of wood and metal and some more gruesome bits, rattled, clattered and spattered on to the ground about us and on to us where we lay.

At length it appeared that the last piece of wreckage had come to earth and, one by one, we struggled to our feet and looked around us. The jetty was gone, destroyed completely, apart from a few torn timbers at the near end, and with it had gone Corese's three henchmen, preferring to end their lives at their own hands than to hang in an English prison.

'They've blown themselves up,' remarked Lestrade, rather unnecessarily I thought.

'That was very clever, Holmes,' I said.

'Not really,' he said. 'We needed cover to get near them, and I recalled that the building further along was a rag store, so I relieved them of some of their rotten stock.'

'What a terrible thing!' said the voice of Father Brennan. 'They had enough on their souls without that,' and he crossed himself and murmured a prayer.

'You need not reproach yourself, Father,' said Holmes. 'You extended every consideration to them.'

'They have died,' said the little cleric, 'steeped in a lifetime's sin – and taken their own lives, which is a great sin in itself. I should have been able to prevent that.'

Shaking his head he trudged away without a word of farewell, dragging his umbrella at his side. Holmes watched him go for a moment, then turned to me.

'Come, Watson,' he said, 'I believe a bath is indicated. Lestrade, will you join us for breakfast?'

I pulled out my watch and realized that the day had hardly begun.

It was a day or two later that I broached with Holmes a matter that had begun to puzzle me. Since the demise of Carella and his friends Holmes had been in a high good humour, which struck me as odd, since he appeared to have failed in the case.

'Holmes,' I ventured, over breakfast one morning, 'do you propose to take any further steps in the Tosca affair?'

'What steps should I take?' he asked, airily. 'Tosca is dead. The right man has been arrested and for the right reason. There will be no prosecution of him, according to Lestrade, because he struck in self-defence and because the Cardinal Archbishop has provided the boy with excellent lawyers. The murderers of Father Grant have chosen their own way out of this world and gone to whatever awaits them. Don Vito Corese has fled abroad, again according to Lestrade. Certainly, if Corese ever sets foot here again I shall seek him out, but apart from that I see no further action that would be necessary or realistic. I would like to hang Corese, but the opportunity may yet arise, and if I do not, Petrosino may yet succeed.'

'What about,' I asked, 'the Vatican Cameos?'

'Ah!' he said. 'The Vatican Cameos. Yes, I should not forget them, but you, Watson, have forgotten Detective Petrosino.'

'Certainly not!' I protested. 'How is he? Do you know?'

'He is very well,' replied Holmes. 'So well that his doctors have passed him fit to travel and he is leaving hospital today. I had thought that we might meet him and take luncheon together.'

Petrosino was waiting for us when we reached the hospital, smartly dressed now that his masquerade was over, in a light summer coat and a straw hat.

His arm was still in a sling and he had a stout stick in his hand, but he walked to our cab without assistance.

'Where are we going?' he asked, as our cabby whipped up the horses.

'We have a short call to make before I am free,' said Holmes, and asked the driver to take us to Victoria Street. I realized that we were on our way to see His Eminence the Cardinal Archbishop of London, but why I could not fathom.

Once inside the Cardinal's Residence we were quickly shown into his presence. He sat behind an imposing desk in a beautifully furnished study, with a wide window at his back. He was formally dressed in the purple and black of his rank. Rising from his chair he greeted Holmes and me warmly, shaking us both by the hand.

'Mr Holmes! Dr Watson! What a very great pleasure, to be sure. It is too long since we met last. The dockers' affair was it not?'

He shook his head, then turned and indicated Petrosino. 'And who have you brought with you, Mr Holmes?'

Holmes introduced the American detective and explained how our paths had crossed. The Cardinal listened with interest.

'And you have succeeded yet again,' he said, when Holmes had done. 'Not only have you traced the murderers of Father Grant, but you saved the unlucky Pisciotto lad from the gallows.'

Holmes inclined his head at the compliment. 'You are most kind,' he said, and looked around him. 'I had hoped,' he continued, 'that before I explained my business here, I might have had the pleasure of seeing Commendatore Lindt again.'

'Ah!' exclaimed His Eminence, regretfully, though his features suggested that the regret was purely formal. 'Commendatore Lindt has had to return to Rome. He was attacked the other night while strolling on the Strand. It appears that his assailant was the madman Cravat. Both were arrested and a little influence was needed to prevent an embarrassment to the Church.'

'Of course,' said Holmes. 'I know that the Commendatore was always anxious to avoid embarrassment to the Church,' and I swear there was no hint of sarcasm in his tone.

The Cardinal nodded. 'Indeed,' he agreed. 'Nevertheless it seemed wise to suggest that he return to his duties at the Vatican. I can, however, express your regrets at missing him next time we are in communication.'

'Please do,' said Holmes, and reached into his coat pocket, producing a stout Manila envelope.

'Your Eminence,' he said. 'My pursuit of the murderers of Father Grant was a personal matter, one in which I engaged because the crime offended me and because I was unsuccessful in taking them years ago.' The Cardinal winced slightly, but said nothing. 'My present enquiry,' Holmes continued, 'however much it has been diverted by other matters, was at the behest of the insurers of the so-called Vatican Cameos. I have come this morning to inform you that I have recovered them, intact, and to present them to you for onward transmission to the Holy Father.'

I think that the jaws of the Cardinal and Petrosino dropped as far as mine at Holmes' words. While we gaped he opened his envelope and extracted five items, laying them in a row upon the red leather top of the Cardinal's desk. Each object was a disc, some two inches in diameter, on which was painted in colours still jewel-bright despite their age, a portrait of an Elizabethan cleric. Each tiny masterpiece was framed in a narrow circlet of twisted gold with a ring at the top.

There was a long silence while all eyes dwelt on the row of little paintings. The Cardinal broke it at last.

'Mr Holmes!' he said. 'How can I ever thank you for returning these treasures of our faith to us? Our Church will be in your debt for ever and His Holiness would grant you anything in return for the preservation of these relics.'

Holmes rose. 'There is no need,' he said. 'If you will confirm to the insurers that I have returned them to your safe keeping I shall be able to submit a note of my fees. That will be quite sufficient.'

We took our luncheon, at Petrosino's suggestion, in an Italian restaurant in Soho, where I sampled a number of unfamiliar but delicious dishes and an excellent wine.

'Holmes,' I said, as I put down my napkin. 'How on earth did you come by the Cameos?'

He smiled. 'You were present, Watson, but it seems you failed to notice.'

'When?' I exclaimed. 'I have never seen them before!'

'I took them,' he said, 'from the pocket of a burglar, outside the Surrey home of Don Vito Corese, a burglar whom we soon learned was our friend Cravat. He had forestalled us and saved us a good deal of trouble and risk.'

'Then you have had them for some time?' I said.

'Of course,' he said, 'but they were never the real purpose of my enquiry.'

I shook my head at this example of the strange intellectual processes of my extraordinary friend.

Days later we saw Petrosino off back to New York. Over the years that followed we heard of his exploits occasionally in the papers and, in 1909, we took dinner with him on an occasion when he passed through London on his way to Sicily. Both Holmes and I were saddened when we heard that, very shortly afterwards, our friend had been shot dead while strolling in a public square in Palermo. It seems that the most likely suspect was Corese, who had returned to his native haunts, but he had, of course, an unshakeable alibi.

The years after Holmes' return from abroad were crammed with some of his most singular cases, but I cannot think of one that outranks in singularity the affair of the Vatican Cameos.

Editor's Notes

I have to tell my readers, with regret, that I cannot assure them with absolute certainty that the present text is really from the pen of John H. Watson. The crucial test of handwriting cannot be made, for we have no proven sample of Watson's script, and there are writers who have demonstrated a regrettable ability to imitate Watson's literary style. All one can hope to do is discover internal evidence in the text that establishes its provenance. Sometimes even that test does not provide proof and one has to be satisfied with the assertion that the text contains nothing which shows it to be a forgery. The notes which follow indicate some of the areas in which I have made checks, and the results of my researches. Others may be able to search longer or more deeply and establish the matter one way or the other.

One
Dr Watson had an unfortunate habit of confusing (whether accidentally or deliberately) the dates of Holmes' cases, but here we can be reasonably sure that the year was 1895. The early weeks of that year were, as he says, bitterly cold, and there was an occasion when the moon showed a greeny-blue tint caused by the weather conditions. It is also the case that the River Thames remained frozen solid well into February, permitting skating and other ice sports. The Northern Lights – the Aurora Borealis – were seen from London, which always provokes rumours that they are an omen of disaster. They are said to have been seen over London in 1939 and they were certainly seen over the Atlantic on the night the *Titanic* sank, their electrical influence probably creating the bad radio conditions of

which operators complained during the rescue efforts. More surprisingly, they were seen by soldiers in the trenches of the Western Front in late June of 1916, only days before the opening of the dreadful battle of the Somme. Perhaps the 1895 sighting of them from London presaged the Jameson Raid and the Second Boer War which sprang from it some years later, though this seems a little too tenuous for a really good omen. The writer has seen them twice – once from Hampshire in 1957 and once from Staffordshire in 1985. On neither occasion do they seem to have heralded any particular disaster.

Most commentators agree that the Affair of the Vatican Cameos, as Watson called it, occurred about 1888. If this is so, then Watson was otherwise engaged, for he was almost certainly courting Mary Morstan who became his wife. A number of commentators have always believed that the Affair of the Vatican Cameos and the Death of Cardinal Tosca might be two different references to the same story, which this narrative (if it is genuine) confirms.

Strictly speaking, as Holmes explains, the Vatican Cameos were not cameos, but miniatures. Cameos were originally silhouettes, moulded or carved in low relief in one colour against a solid background of another colour, a technique used to decorate everything from personal jewellery to walls. The term came, however, to mean anything small and perfect in art.

Two

The mention of Adam Worth and Professor Moriarty in the same conversation is astonishing. For many years, commentators have asserted that Adam Worth was the real original of Moriarty – indeed, Holmes referred to Moriarty as the 'Napoleon of Crime', a title which was also applied to Worth. Nevertheless, here we have Holmes and Watson discussing the two villains as separate individuals.

Adam Worth was a German Jew born in America, who,

in the early stages of the American Civil War, was listed among the dead. This so encouraged him that he embarked upon a long career of crime, organizing robberies and frauds in America, Britain, Europe, Africa and the Middle East without getting caught for years. He is estimated to have stolen as much as $3,000,000 during his career, but his most famous exploit was the theft of Gainsborough's portrait of the Duchess of Devonshire (then the most costly painting in the world) from Agnew's showroom in Old Bond Street, London, in May 1876. This was not done for profit. He kept the portrait to himself for many years (even sleeping with it according to legend) perhaps because it bears a strong resemblance to the great lost love of his life. Captured at last in France, he was sentenced to imprisonment for an attempt to rob a railway freight car. The sentence seems to have broken his spirit and his health. He emerged from jail penniless and, at long last, made an arrangement to return the Devonshire portrait for a price. He came to London to see it displayed and died within days.

Holmes called Moriarty the 'Napoleon of Crime', as Scotland Yard nicknamed Worth. It is that nickname that has led many commentators to believe that Moriarty is a fictitious version of Worth. Indeed, the only biography of Worth adopts the nickname – *The Napoleon of Crime: The Life and Times of Adam Worth, Master Thief* (Ben Macintyre, Farrar, Straus & Giroux, New York, 1997) and asserts that Worth is the original Moriarty.

If the present narrative is a forgery, one would have imagined that the forger would have adopted the popular view that Worth and Moriarty are one, rather than drawing attention to their differences. What is more, if they are not one, that leaves us the fascinating question of who Professor Moriarty really was!

Holmes' lecture on the history of insurance is largely correct. The original insurers were little more than sophisticated protection racketeers.

Three

The word 'diklo' means a neckerchief and derives from the Romani language of Gypsies.

The threatening of small businesses by poisoning tradesmen's horses was a method employed by the protection gangs in New York around this period.

Four

Edward II died just as Holmes describes. Held prisoner by his enemies in Berkeley Castle, Gloucestershire, he was first put in a cell near the castle's sewer, in the hope that he would develop a fatal infection from the atmosphere. When this failed, his captors assassinated him in the way Holmes indicates, so that they could display his unmarked corpse and claim that they had done him no harm. The method of execution is thought also to have been a sardonic comment on Edward's sexual preferences.

Five

There is at least one tea merchant in Britain whose premises are still like Watson's description of Greenfrew and Massley's shop. In Queen Street, Wolverhampton, is Snapes', a dealer in tea and coffee, whose premises scent the entire street. There you may see the giant canisters blazoned in gold and bright colours and there you may witness the astonishing skill of the counter assistants in weighing, wrapping and tying packets of loose tea faster than the eye can follow. On at least two occasions ladies from Snapes' shop have appeared on *The Generation Game* show, challenging contestants to emulate their skills.

Mr Greenfrew was horrified by Watson's account of Indian tea-making. He would be equally horrified by modern English tea-making with the milk put in the cup first. Until World War Two, this method was referred to scornfully as 'American' or 'French' tea. Secret agents sent into Occupied France had to be trained to do it, so as not to give themselves away.

Nowadays the practice has become widespread in Britain, despite the fact that, by scalding the milk with hot tea, the flavour is changed out of recognition.

Six

Lestrade calls Petrosino a 'hurdy-gurdy grinder', which is not correct. A hurdy-gurdy was (and is) an instrument once played all over the Continent in which violin-like strings are played not with a bow but with a rotating wheel driven by a hand-turned handle. Despite the difference, when the barrel organ appeared on Britain's streets, it was quite often known as a hurdy-gurdy.

The Commissioner Roosevelt mentioned will have been Theodore Roosevelt, sometime New York's Commissioner of Police, but better known as President of the United States and the man who gave his name to the 'Teddy' bear.

The story of the Jewish police detective who had never seen a crucifix is true.

Giuseppe (Joseph) Petrosino was a real character. Born in Salerno, Italy, in 1860, he travelled with his family to the USA in 1873. His initial connection with the Police Department was as an informer, helping the largely Irish police force to deal with crime among Italian immigrants. In 1883 he became a uniformed officer, but by cultivating a friendship with Commissioner Roosevelt he was eventually freed of all duties other than 'unusual cases' and authorized to work in plain clothes.

Pursuing a lifelong career against the Italian gangs, he held views similar to those that Watson attributes to him. He was murdered in Sicily in 1909 (see note to final chapter).

It is true that Petrosino means 'parsley' in some Southern Italian dialects and provided a nickname and a warning cry against him. If he was spotted about a criminous area, the cry 'I have parsley!' would be raised, and his becoming a policeman was greeted with the joke that parsley might make the Police Department taste better, but it would always be indigestible. His colleagues in the Homicide Squad knew him as 'the Dago', the press took to calling him 'the Detective in the Derby', because of his taste in high-crowned Derby hats.

Seven
Petrosino was always contemptuous of the Italian gangs, pointing out that the name 'Black Hand' predated large-scale Italian migration to New York and had been used by others. While he recognized the existence of the Mafia, he knew that it was not all-embracing or all-powerful, but one of a wide range of criminal organizations in the USA, which included gangs of many nationalities.

The Rules he quotes as belonging to the Rule of Nine are very similar to a set recovered by the US Secret Service from a Black Hand member about 1900.

Eight
Petrosino is right about Irish immigrants creating a power base in nineteenth-century Boston. Among the families involved in Boston Irish politics were the Fitzgeralds and the Kennedys, who were the ancestors of President John F. Kennedy. The President's father, Joseph Kennedy, once recalled that, as a boy, he had seen two of his father's supporters arrive on an election day and reported that each had voted more than one hundred and twenty times!

The reference to 'the French days' is, apparently, a reference to the period when Sicily was part of the twin kingdoms of Sicily and Naples, ruled by the French Angevin Kings. It is said that the Mafia was born in those days as an anti-French resistance movement.

Nine
Sherlock Holmes is correct in stating that Britain was

formally a Christian land long before Pope Gregory sent Augustine here. Britain was a province of the Roman Empire until AD 410. Rome became Christian in AD 326, so Britain had nearly a century of official Christianity before the Romans withdrew. It was more than two and a half centuries after Britain was Christianized that Augustine was sent to convert Celtic Christians to Roman Christians. Subsequently Henry VIII split with the Pope and appointed himself head of an English Catholic Church, turned into the Protestant Church of England by his daughter Elizabeth.

Eleven
'Hokey pokey' was a form of water ice, sold from street vendors' carts to the cry, 'Hokey pokey, penny a lump!'

Twelve
Italian-American gangsters living in wealthy seclusion in rural Surrey? It all sounds very unlikely, and I cannot confirm that it ever happened in the 1890s. Historians, policemen and journalists have argued for years about whether or when organized crime had imported itself from the USA to Britain. There have certainly been odd incursions over the years. For example, James Hynes, an associate of 'Legs' Diamond, was injured in a shootout with the FBI and hospitalized in the USA. He escaped to Britain and started operations here, though he could not understand the unwillingness of British villains to carry firearms. In 1937 he was caught and sentenced for robberies, dying a few years later in an English prison. Now we know, to our cost, that we have representatives of organized crime from many nations operating in these islands. David Rose, in *In the Name of the Law: The Collapse of Criminal Justice* (Jonathan Cape, London 1996), refers to Sicilian Francesco di Carlo, jailed for twenty-five years in 1987 for importing drugs. Rose describes him as living 'in splendour amid the "stockbroker belt" in Woking, Surrey', and goes on:

His wife was active in local charities, and his neighbours believed that the dapper individual who left for London on the commuter trains each morning worked in the hotel business. Di Carlo did indeed own hotels and other 'straight' commercial interests, but his main business was the import of heroin and cannabis.

His neighbours were also unaware that he was wanted in Italy for helping to plan the 1983 murder of General Dalla Chiesa, an anti-terrorist expert sent by Rome to fight the Mafia. In fact, di Carlo and other fugitives from Italian justice had set up a special Mafia cell in Surrey. An even more senior Cosa Nostra figure, Alfonse Caruana, lived a few miles away from di Carlo, near Charterhouse School, in a £450,000 mansion, and his brother, Pasquale, occupied a house worth £350,000 on the other side of Woking. Both men fled once di Carlo was arrested. Their money-laundering operation stretched from Hong Kong to East Africa, taking in banks in the Bahamas, Tokyo, Vienna, New York, London and small High Street branches in the West Country.

If it can happen today, I imagine it would have been a great deal easier a century ago.

Nineteen
Holmes' reference to Baroness Coutts must be to Baroness Burdett-Coutts, a friend of Charles Dickens and a wealthy philanthropist very much concerned with the urban poor. She is remembered today for her experiments in providing good, cheap housing for the poor which was also profitable to landlords, but she should be honoured for another reason as well. She sought the advice of dieticians on the eating habits of Victorian slum dwellers, who bought their cooked food, when they could afford it, from fried fish or hot potato shops. Her experts pointed out that a combination of the two would be a pretty reasonably balanced

meal and she began persuading the shopkeepers to combine their output, giving birth to the British national dish – fish and chips!

Twenty-Two
The description of 'Father Brennan' will seem familiar to readers of G. K. Chesterton's 'Father Brown' stories, which poses another question. Is Watson disguising Father Brown as Father Brennan or was Father Brown's name really Brennan? Or is this merely a monstrous coincidence?

Twenty-Five
Diabolos were a favourite Victorian toy, consisting of a cylindrical object with a narrow waist which was kept spinning on a length of cord stretched between the hands. Teetotums were (and are) the six-sided spinners used as a substitute for dice in board games.

It is the case that backstreet workshops in Birmingham provided a wide range of toys, novelties and ornaments to be used all over the Empire as 'trade goods' and sold worldwide. A century ago most of the Jews' harps used anywhere were made in Brum. Now no one in Britain makes them. In the 1960s I spent an afternoon at such a workshop in Aston, though it had ceased to trade many years before. The owner told me how his father and he would supply tin goods to the de Beers company for the African trade in the 1920s. He also told me that his father had invented the ever-popular musical kazoo during the Great War, when he marketed it as a short-term novelty called 'The Musical Submarine' and never bothered to patent it. At the time that I met him there were plastic kazoos on sale all over Britain and nobody manufacturing tin ones any more.

Twenty-Eight
'Keeping obbo' is an old (and still current) police abbreviation for 'keeping observation'.

Twenty-Nine

Where did Holmes and Watson meet Cardinal Manning? It seems, from the Cardinal's remark, that it had some connection with the great Dock Strike of 1889, in which His Eminence intervened on the side of the dockers. One hopes that the story may yet come to light.

Petrosino died as Watson describes. He had gone to Sicily (at his own expense) in an attempt to persuade the authorities there to co-operate with the New York Police. The local investigation into his murder fizzled out inconclusively, but in 1911 Giuseppe Morello, former head of the Black Hand in New York, revealed while in Atlanta prison that Petrosino's death had been the work of Vito Cascio Ferro. Two gangsters who had fled from America back to Sicily believed that Petrosino had come to capture them. They sought Don Vito's help and he, personally, lured the detective into a trap and killed him. During World War Two, Cascio Ferro himself confessed to the murder, but nothing was done. Mussolini had just appointed Don Vito Genovese as a Knight of the Realm and America was looking for Mafia help in the landings on Sicily and in Italy.

If Petrosino never nailed 'Corese', it seems likely that the name hides the identity of Don Vito Cascio Ferro, who eventually came to an extraordinary and horrible end. In the 1920s Sicily was subjected to a ruthless anti-Mafia campaign under Prefect Mori and Ferro was convicted in 1930 of complicity in two murders. He was sentenced to nine years' imprisonment.

Don Vito was a prisoner in Pozzuoli penitentiary in 1943, when Fascist Italy collapsed under Allied invasion and bombing. The surviving authorities ordered the evacuation of Pozzuoli's prisoners and they were removed, with the exception of eighty-one-year-old Don Vito Cascio Ferro. By accident (?) he was overlooked during the evacuation of the prison and died alone of thirst in his cell in the abandoned penitentiary.

199

There is an excellent biography of Petrosino, *Joe Petrosino*, by Arrigo Petacco, translated by Charles Markmann (London, Hamish Hamilton, 1974). There is also a biopic, *Pay or Die*, in which he was played by Ernest Borgnine.

None of the above points establish conclusively that the present text is authentic, however. I leave the matter to the reader's own decision and any researches he chooses to carry out, remarking only that the conversation about Adam Worth strongly suggests that the manuscript is not a forgery.

Barrie Roberts
June 2003